KFIR LUZZATTO

I0552215

DEAD & BUSY

EPISODES 1-4

PINE TEN

Pine Ten, LLC
205 North Michigan Avenue
Chicago, IL 60601

ISBN: 978-1-938212-52-9

Table of Contents

EPISODE ONE

ACCIDENTAL LAZARUS

CHAPTER 1

Drip, drip ... Drip, drip ...

The sound was coming from my best armchair, the one I like to sit in to watch the game. I stood, flabbergasted, gaping at Joe Murray, alias Giovanni di Mare, aka Stupid Joe (although you never called him so to his face). Stupid Joe was a mobster, well known in his neighborhood for the easy, nonchalant way in which he handled those who fell in disgrace with his family. If you dug deep enough, he was not a bad sort. I had often had a beer with him when fishing for information and from time to time he had given me useful tips. He got around and knew a lot about what was going on in his circles, but as his nickname suggested, he was not an owl.

Stupid Joe was holding a whacking big pistol in one hand, and a glass in the other. Judging by the bottle on the table next to him, what he was drinking was the low-quality Scotch with which I always fill a bottle of the best label. That is the whiskey that I offer my guests, who anyway can't tell the difference between petrol and the finest Scotch on earth. He was directing me to the chair in front of him with a friendly movement of his gun. I, on the other hand, was too amazed to move. It was not the fact that Stupid Joe had broken into my apartment that had left me speechless—when you are a private eye it's an occupational hazard—nor was the fact that he was drinking my whiskey that left me perplexed. Even his pointing a gun at me was not the reason for freezing as I did (I have had guns of all kinds pointed at me by assorted goons over the years, and one gets used to it). But I had been watching the news at my girlfriend's house the night before, and that's why I was spooked beyond words.

If you are like me, I'm sure that much of what they feed you in the news sounds unclear, wrong, or plainly a lie. But this time the news had been very clear about one thing: One Mafioso known as Joe Murray, they said, had been shot in the back in a busy bar. The gun employed to rid the world of this scourge of humanity, they explained in lavish details, was a big caliber hunting rifle that had bored an impressively large hole in Joe's back, and had left an even larger exit wound in his chest—one through which you could easily poke your head.

The identity of the murderer wasn't known, and the police were making inquiries. I bet they were. I could almost hear the sigh of ecstasy let out by those who, now that Stupid Joe had checked out and was lying on a slab at the morgue, felt that the world had suddenly become a better and a safer place for them to live in.

Only he wasn't lying on any damn slab, if you follow me. He was in my living room, sitting in my armchair and drinking my whiskey. He did look a little pale though, as befitting one who had been clinically dead for a while, but apart from that you wouldn't have thought that anything was wrong with him. If you overlooked the hole, that is.

At this point you may wonder how come I didn't faint, freak out and lose it. Well, truth is that, apart from the first shock, the visit I was having was not entirely unusual for me. Stop me if you've heard this before—I'm not sure if you're familiar with what I do— but I'm quite well known as a paranormal detective. I'm not bragging, just stating a fact. In a nutshell, that means that I can see dead people that you may not be able to see, and they have a tendency of flocking around me. That's my gift, or as some people would say, my curse. It is sort of annoying having deadies dropping by at all hours, but on the other hand that's how I make a living, so I can't complain. Nevertheless, this Stupid Joe was a novelty item, because up to that point my visitors had been incorporeal, while he was plainly here in the flesh.

Joe was wearing a raincoat two sizes too small for him—he was a big guy, more or less my size, to give you an idea—which he had left unbuttoned. Other than that, he wore only a pair of dirty shorts. His feet were crammed into tight sneakers. The hole in his chest that had been so widely advertised on TV was even larger than I had imagined. The shot had apparently taken out an entire length of his esophagus, and drops of my precious Scotch were falling from its severed end, onto the rim of the carbonized exit hole, which accounted for the dripping sound. From the edge of the exit wound they flew out and splashed onto the cushion of my armchair. Every time he took a sip the stream of drops intensified, and the drip ... drip ... drip ... quickened. I was hypnotized by that dripping hole and wasn't able to take my eyes off it.

"Take a seat, Dave," he said to me in a low, rasping voice, once again pointing helpfully to the chair with the gun. "I'd hate to have to whack you."

"Hi, Joe," I said, regaining some of my composure at the sound of his voice. It was not a beautiful voice, but it was as human as it had always been. "I'd heard reports ..."

"That someone had whacked me, right?" He rubbed his right ear with the muzzle of the gun and made a face.

"Right. And you do look a little the worse for wear, I must say—no offense meant," I hastened to add. You didn't offend Stupid Joe, if you wanted to see the next sunrise standing up.

"Yeah, it stinks. Do you want to hear what happened? Of course you want to hear what happened. I am at the Blue Bird bar, you know, the one downtown where they have this new number with this girl curling up ... have you seen it?"

"No, I haven't, but I know the place you're talking about. It was in the news."

"You should go and see it. It's unbelievable what this girl can do ... but that's not the point now. The point is, I am there, talking to a broad and passing the time of day, when I hear a shout and a shot, and the next thing I know, I wake up on a slab at the morgue, really pissed off, you know."

"You woke up? How did that happen?"

"I have no idea. I just did. At first I couldn't remember what had happened to me, but after a minute it all came back."

"And they simply let you go?" I mean, how sloppy can the morgue's personnel be?

"Nobody was around to stop me. I looked for someone, but it was dead bodies all over. The place was empty at this time of night, otherwise I would have whacked somebody just to feel alive again. SIT DOWN!" he boomed when I instinctively got up.

"No need to get excited," I said. "I'm not going anywhere. But I'm glad you didn't find anybody to whack. Whacking someone who's not involved in what happened to you wouldn't be nice," I added.

"It would be a relief, though. I may still do it. Anyway, I'm on this slab and I sit up and start thinking what to do about it. I'm naked, you see, and I can't go out like that. So I look around until I find this stuff I am wearing now, and then I figure I should come and talk to you."

"Why me? Why don't you talk to the police? They're investigating right now, and I am sure they'll find the person who did this to you, in no time."

"Bah! The police couldn't find your dog's shit if it left it under the lamp in front of the police station. No, everybody knows that Dave Callaghan is the best private eye there is, so it's you who is going to find this guy for me, so that I can get even with him."

It appeared that I was being engaged, and wasn't getting to say no. Still, it was worth trying . . .

"But, Joe, I don't think you have any money now. How will you be paying for the investigation? I mean, I like you, and I am sorry for you, but I never work unless there is something in it for me."

"But you stand to gain from it too."

"Yeah, what?"

"Well, if you find him, I won't whack you. That's fair enough, I think."

That was Stupid Joe in a nutshell. A sudden thought occurred to me.

"Sorry for asking, but you *are* dead, right?"

"I guess so. I can't tell you how sore I am because of it. But I'm pretty sure that I'm dead. I'm dead cold. Here," he said, pointing at his arm, "feel my flesh. I'm cold and no pulse. FEEL MY FLESH, I SAID!" he ordered, when I made a polite gesture declining the invitation.

Well, it did feel cold. And there was no pulse. He was dead all right, but somehow his brain had not yet caught up with it, and refused to stop commanding the body. Perhaps the amount of intellect involved in running Stupid Joe's business was so minimal that it could go on, at least for a while, even after his death. I've seen that happening before, but usually only for a few minutes before the machinery gave up. With Stupid Joe it seemed like he would go on forever. Still, I had to find a way to make him realize his situation if I wanted to get rid of him any time soon.

"Yeah," I agreed, "you are as dead as they come. Look here," I added, trying to bring our little discussion onto a more businesslike plane, "I'm ready to help you find who did this to you, on one condition."

"I didn't say anything about allowing conditions, but shoot anyway."

"My condition is that the moment we find this guy and you get even with him, you go straight back to your nice slab at the morgue, where you belong, and let nature take its course. Do we have a deal?"

"Oh, I don't know."

"But Joe, be reasonable. You came to me because I'm good and you want me to find this guy. But to do a good job I need motivation. If you can't pay for my work, you must at last give me your word that once I deliver, we're done. That's motivation enough for me to find him."

Stupid Joe's countenance became one of deep thought, meaning that he looked like a badly cut marble statue forgotten in someone's junkyard. After a while, he lowered his gaze, which he had directed to a light switch at the other end of the room, and nodded.

"OK. You have my word. I promise that as soon as I'm through working on this guy you're going to find for me, I'll go back to the morgue and you'll never hear from me again."

"It's a deal, then."

"Yeah. No more chin wagging now," ordered Joe. "How are we going to start this investigation?"

"We? You have no part in any investigation. I'm the detective, remember?"

"We are a team," said Joe, speaking softly.

"No, we aren't. This is detective work, not team work."

"WE ARE A TEAM, I SAID!" Joe boomed again. I realized

that arguing wouldn't do me any good. I had to play ball, at least until I discovered who the shooter was, or I found another way to get rid of Joe.

"Well," I said, resigned, "then we must get organized. First of all, we need to get you some decent clothing. You are more or less my size. Come here," I said, moving toward my small bedroom, "I'll find something that fits you."

I looked into my closet and selected a suit that I had always thought too bright for me, and matched it with a pair of shoes, socks, and a dress shirt with a tie. I had let a former girlfriend talk me into buying that suit, and the next week we had a row that ended it, so I never had to wear it.

Soon it became clear that we had a problem, though: the liquid oozing out of the hole in Joe's chest would drench the shirt and suit in no time.

"Here," I said, handing him a towel. "Stuff that into that hole, to stop the liquid from wetting everything." I watched him do it and, encouraged by his apparent docility, I asked, "Why do you go on drinking, anyway? Do you taste the stuff at all?"

"To tell you the truth, no. I'm kinda unable to taste anything. It's just the habit. I can stop drinking, if you prefer it."

"I do. Yes, I definitely prefer it. It's not that I'm begrudging you the booze, but we need to avoid being conspicuous, and if you come around with me spilling Scotch from your chest, it doesn't help that."

"OK," he said quietly. Joe now seemed much more manageable than I had ever seen him—pensive, is the word I was grasping for, and one never associated Joe with thought. Perhaps death softens the toughest guys, though.

I felt sorry for him—but not half as sorry as for myself. If I wanted this nightmare to end, I realized, we'd better start getting busy.

"Let's begin by going to the Blue Bird. You'll need a disguise—we don't want anybody to recognize you and to freak out. Here," I said, pushing a false beard and mustache at him, "paste this on your face. The mirror is over there."

The result was quite impressive, I must say. The shop where I buy my disguise gear is very good, and even I wouldn't have recognized him with that beard. We left the apartment and went down the flight of stairs to the car park. He walked a little strangely, in a sort of side-to-side wobbly fashion, but overall, he looked quite normal. When we reached my car, he extended an open hand.

"The keys," he said curtly.

"What!"

"You heard me. Gimme the keys."

If you know me, you have heard that the one thing I love more than my mother is my shiny, blue Jaguar. It's the apple of my eye and you're not allowed to eat, drink, or smoke in it. Above all, nobody—and I mean *nobody*—besides me drives it. I panicked.

"But you can't drive," I pleaded. "I don't trust your reflexes, and your driving license expired by law when you legally died." I was looking for excuses, *any* excuse, to keep him from driving my Jaguar. "And you smell of whiskey—the whole towel is soaked with it—so what do we do if a policeman stops us while you drive?"

"Simple, we whack him and go on."

Joe's simple logic was hard to defeat, but I didn't give up.

"Now you listen to me, Joe. You can't go around whacking people. Particularly police officers. Someone is bound to take notice, and it may get in the way of our investigation. You must correct this tendency of yours to whack everybody in sight. Forget it, expunge it from your thoughts!"

"All right. Now gimme the keys."

"Sorry. You don't get to drive my Jaguar, and that's final!"

This is why we were now driving at twice the speed limit along Rosebud Boulevard with Joe at the wheel and me trying to remember whether I had mailed the check to the insurance company. We finally reached the Blue Bird, and not a moment too soon. Joe parked the car right in front of the entrance to the bar, which was swell since it improved our chances of finding it again when we came out, and we moved toward the door.

"Let me do all the talking," I commanded, before we went in. "While we are on the job, I'm the boss. Agreed?"

"Agreed. You are the boss. Now move your ass and get down to work."

The atmosphere in the bar was merry and noisy. You wouldn't have believed that only a few hours earlier someone had been shot dead in that very spot. The lights were dim, and the air was full of smoke, but the place was packed with happy couples and singles. We approached the bar and the barman greeted us with a smile.

"What will it be, gentlemen?"

"Scotch for me," I said, "and nothing for my friend."

"Scotch for me too," said Joe, and then whispered to me with a wink: "I've stuffed in an extra towel for that." He patted me on the back with a camaraderie that was out of character for him and his arm pushed me so hard that I bumped into the bar.

"Hey!" I complained. "Cut it out! You're gonna crack me a rib or something."

"Sorry," he said with a grin that didn't look at all apologetic. "I find it difficult to control my strength now that I can't feel a thing. Hey, look!" he added, sounding excited. "That's the girl, the one with the curling up number. I have a mind to go and talk to her."

"I'd rather you stayed put and talked to nobody," I said, speaking severely and hoping that my tone would drive it home.

"I'm going up to the manager's office to make inquiries. Wait for me here and don't get into any trouble."

"Yeah, yeah," he answered, his eyes fixed on the girl, but he plainly wasn't listening.

I left him to his gazing exercise. No harm done there, I assumed.

On my way up I worked on my line of inquiry. I knew the manager slightly, and wasn't expecting much cooperation. That was lucky, 'cause I got none. William McIntire, better known as "Flash Billy," on account of his skill at cheating with cards, was sitting behind a dirty desk, eating a salami sandwich, a can of beer in his other hand. Fat was dripping from the side of his mouth and the sight was revolting.

"Hi, Billy," I said genially, when I let myself in without knocking, "how are you these days?"

"I'm fine," he mumbled out of a full mouth. "Beat it."

"Not so quick, Billy. Just a few questions and I'll leave you to you gourmet dinner."

He gave me a scornful look.

"Why should I take any questions from you?" he said at last. "What are you, the police commissioner?"

"Nope. But I have an interest in what happened to Stupid Joe here, yesterday, and I need some information from you."

"Why is that any business of yours? And why do you care?" he mumbled through a full mouth. He swallowed some, made a dismissive gesture with his can of beer, and added, "Good riddance to bad rubbish, I say."

"I wouldn't say that out loud if I were you," I warned him. I worried that Joe might be within earshot. With his tendency to go about whacking people at the slightest provocation, we might end the day with another corpse.

"You're not me, thank God!" he said, quite offensively, "and I don't give a shit about Stupid Joe or you, for that matter. I don't know why you're sticking your nose into other people's business, and I don't care."

"Take it from me that I have an interest—it doesn't matter why—and I need to hear from you what you know about it."

"Nothing."

"Nothing?"

"Nothing. Not a word. I have nothing for you. Now beat it."

Billy went back to work again on his sandwich as if I wasn't there. Clearly, he wasn't going to tell me anything. It was quite a disgusting scene, so I left without closing the door behind me. He would have to get up to shut it and I was at least that much ahead of the game.

I climbed down the stairs, feeling at a dead end. I had hoped to get something to start working on from people at the bar, but since that wasn't going to happen I didn't know where to start to investigate the shooting. Perhaps the best plan would be to start with Stupid Joe. He might have information that he didn't realize he should tell me. Yes, that definitely was the way to go. I had to start working with Joe right away.

But Joe was gone. The bar was crowded with people of every color, age, and size—but no Joe. He was nowhere in sight. Nor, I noticed, was the girl with the "curling act."

CHAPTER 2

I had made the fatal mistake of leaving the car keys with Joe. I ran outside and saw with horror that my Jaguar was gone. And it wasn't the only thing gone—my wallet wasn't in my breast pocket where I had put it. All that friendly pat-on-the-back act had been a trick and I had let Stupid Joe pickpocket me. You can't beat that for stupidity. If word got around that I had been tricked like a tenderfoot by an awkward zombie, my reputation would be ruined.

It took me three hours to walk home from the bar, because I needed to find Joe before he got himself, and by reflex me, into serious trouble. I looked everywhere, but of course he was nowhere to be found so I finally gave up and headed for home. I opened the door of my apartment with a bowed head and sore feet. Someone was in my living room, which, I thought bitterly, appeared to be no longer my private place, since people were always dropping in without asking first. At first I was relieved to see that Lizzy—my girlfriend—was sitting at one end of the couch.

Let me tell you about my Elizabeth—Lizzy to her friends. I had been going out with Lizzy for five months now, and I really liked her. Her only defect was her intellectual side—she worked as a guide at the Museum of Modern Arts and was on a crusade to better me. She expected me to go all ecstatic at the sight of a dirty canvas onto which some slob had thrown the yolk of an egg, if you get me, and things like that. She also wanted me to read books—not the good kind, with a bit of blood and a few corpses thrown in, but the kind of books with pictures of stuff that is supposed to be inspiring. Most of the time if you ask me what they are about, I have no clue. I had learned how to steer her away from her pet subjects, though, and more often than not I was able to keep art out of the conversation.

She had the keys to my apartment so it was okay for her to be there, but I immediately realized that she wasn't alone. Deep in conversation with Lizzy, at the other end of the couch and sporting my silk pajamas (a present from a former girlfriend) was Stupid Joe, false beard and all. My girlfriend was chatting with a dead mobster who, at any given moment, might double over and, finally, check out. How much weirder can it get? The thought of Lizzy finding out who ... what she was talking to sent a chill along my spine.

"Hi, Dave," said Lizzy, jumping up as she saw me coming in, "we've been waiting for you. Where have you been all this time?"

"I had work to do," I mumbled, eyeing Joe. I couldn't figure out what was going on, but I had to find a way to get Lizzy out of there and now wasn't soon enough.

"You never told me about your friend Gustave," she said reproachfully.

"Gustave?" I had no idea what she was talking about. "What about him?"

"I had a wonderful chat with Gustave while you were away and learned that you are good friends. You never tell me about your friends," she complained.

How Stupid Joe had morphed into a Gustave was more than I could fathom, but that was the wrong time to inquire.

"Uh-huh, we go back a long time," I said between clenched teeth, frowning at Joe at the same time—not an easy thing to do, I can tell you that.

Joe lifted his eyebrows with a schoolgirl-like smile, ill-fitted to his ugly features, and shrugged his shoulders in an apologetic gesture.

"Well, I seldom come to town, you know," he said to Lizzy, and then turning to me he added, "I'm sorry for not giving you advance notice, but I phoned and couldn't find you. Is this a bad time? Am I in the way?"

"As a matter of fact, this is not a good time. I'm in the middle of a case," I said. I couldn't kick Lizzy out, but I hoped that Joe would have enough sense to understand that I wanted him to go, wait for Lizzy to leave, and then come back.

Not a chance, of course.

"Nonsense!" Lizzy ruled sharply. "Of course you'll put Gustave up for the night."

"But, you see, this is complicated ..."

"Well, he can't sleep in the street," she said curtly. She tends to be bossy and God knows why I put up with that. "If he can't stay with you, I'll invite him to my place," she added, knowing very well that I would cave in.

"No, no. It's OK, I'll manage," I answered quickly. I only wanted Lizzy to leave before matters became more complicated than they already were.

"Is it OK for me to sleep on the couch?" asked Joe, so politely that I had to take a second look to make sure that he was the one speaking. The seraphic smile that he had pasted on his face was starting to get on my nerves.

"Yes, yes. OK. Come on, I'll give you a pillow and a blanket," I said hastily. I wanted Joe to myself, and I wanted an explanation.

"I'll make some coffee while you organize," said Lizzy.

"Not for me, thank you," said Joe. "I can't sleep well after coffee."

Thank God he has some sense left in him, I thought with relief.

Black coffee gurgling out of his hole and onto my white silk pajamas would give rise to questions.

"What do you mean, disappearing on me like that?" I whispered angrily, once I managed to close the door of my bedroom behind us. "I told you to stay put and out of trouble. Where have you been? How did you get here?"

"Yes, yes. You're right. I'm sorry. But, you see, I got into conversation with that girl down at the bar—you should really see her curling act—and I couldn't help myself. I told her: 'Let's get out of here, what do you think?' and she said: 'Your place or mine?' So we went to her place."

"And ..." Speaking about curling, I could feel the hair curling on the back of my neck.

"And we spoke of this and of that for a while, then we had something to drink, and I started to leak. Then she said, 'Oh, look, you've spilled your drink on your shirt. Let me take care of that.' And I know that it was really stupid of me ..."

"What! You didn't!"

"Ahem, yes, I did. I let her take off my shirt."

"And ..." I prompted him again, feeling weak at the knees.

"Well, I hope she has come to, by now. When I left her, she was gone, though. She gave a little cry and fainted. That was it. I don't know why; you didn't faint."

I didn't tell him that I almost did. There was no point.

"So now she's probably telling everybody about you, and they'll be looking for you. What were you thinking? What was the big idea?"

I was really pissed off. Not only was I in this against my will and better judgment, but he was also doing everything in his power to make life more difficult for me.

"I'm sorry," said Joe. He looked sincerely apologetic, and I couldn't help feeling sad for him. On the other hand, there are times when you need to play your hand well and take advantage of the situation, and that was one of those times.

"You know that I have a good mind to call the whole thing off?" I said, gazing at him carefully to gauge his reaction—not an easy thing to do when you're talking to an expressionless cadaver. "I agreed to help you, but if you keep interfering with my investigation, there is nothing more that I can do for you."

"Please, Dave ... I'll be good, I promise."

I looked at him. He had started talking like a scolded child. I wondered if he was regressing into childhood. Perhaps he was undergoing some kind of progressive death. Still, I liked this new and improved Joe better. He was much more manageable than before.

"Yeah, OK," I said curtly, "but no more funny ideas, OK?"

"OK."

"Now my wallet," I said, putting out a hand.

"Your what?"

His pretense of innocence was pathetic.

"The wallet you picked from my pocket. Now," I said.

"Oh, is this yours?" he asked, producing it from his pocket. "I found it near the bar when you went up and I don't know how it happened to be there."

I checked it. A hundred bucks were missing, but I said nothing. What was the point? But there was something else that had bothered me since the moment I walked in.

"How did you pick that ridiculous name, Gustave?" I asked.

"Well, you see, I knew that I needed a name—I mean, one that was not my own—and I couldn't think of a good one when she asked. I didn't have much time to think and I saw a book by Gustave Miller on your shelf, so I told her that Gustave was my name."

I knew the book to which he referred. It was a present from Lizzy and was entitled *My Fjord—Chronicle of Nature's Art*. I only kept it on my shelf out of necessity, but was in perpetual fear that one of my friends might see it and get a good laugh at my expense. I made a mental note to hide it behind some other book as soon as Lizzy wasn't around.

We went back to the living room with a pillow and bed sheets—acting it out for Lizzy's benefit. I didn't think that Joe really needed them. The coffee was on the table and Lizzy was standing.

"I'm tired and it's late," she said. "I think that I'll go home. It was great talking to you, Gustave. Good night."

"Good night, Elizabeth. Conversing with you was an exquisite experience. It was charming."

I gazed at him sideways. I'm sure he never used words like "charming and "exquisite" before. Lizzy was apparently having a deep, debilitating effect on him. I turned to her.

"I'll walk you to your car," I said. I wasn't being chivalrous. I needed to find out what nonsense Joe had been telling her. At the door she turned to Joe.

"I'll pick you up at nine, then," she said, and walked out.

I closed the door behind us and, trying to sound natural, I asked her, "What was that about picking him up at nine?"

"Oh, nothing. Gustave has never been to the Modern Arts Museum, so I offered to take him."

That was a good one. A stupid mobster spending quality time at the museum.

"Really, you don't have to go to all that trouble."

"But I want to. He's your friend, and he's nice. He's so big and awkward, and at the same time so cute."

"Cute!" I almost yelled. Nobody ever thought of Stupid Joe as "cute"; "spooky" was more like it.

"Well, well," said Lizzy, giving me a strange look, "are we being jealous?"

"Me, jealous? Not at all. Why?" I asked, feeling a sudden knot in my stomach, "Did he come on to you?"

"You *are* jealous!" she said with a little laugh. "Of course not, you silly. He's a friend of yours, isn't he?"

I mumbled something unclear in response. We had reached her car and I stood beside her while she opened it. She kissed me hurriedly and got inside. Then she opened the window and poked her head out.

"By the way, Dave. Don't you ever air your apartment? There was a rancid smell in there, as if you kept spoiled food in your living room. I would open a window every now and then, if I were you."

Without waiting for an answer she waved to me brightly, and was gone.

I walked back to my apartment, trying to figure out whether I was ready to pick a fight with Joe. But when I walked into the apartment he was sitting on the couch, reading the most recent issue of the *National Geographic* magazine, and I didn't have the heart.

I took a long shower and, before going to sleep, I opened the door to my living room to see what Joe was up to. He was still sitting there, with the magazine in his hands. I closed the door silently and stretched out on the bed. I'd had enough of Joe for the day and if he was keeping himself busy without my help, it was all right with me.

CHAPTER 3

I normally fall asleep as soon as I hit the hay and sleep a dreamless sleep for eight straight hours, but I have to admit that this time I had a restless night, waking up every hour or so to check on Joe. You see, I have this damn habit, when I'm on a job, of making a list of all the dangers I may have to face, to prepare for them, and it had occurred to me that Joe might suddenly go berserk and murder me in my sleep. I had no idea what changes might take place in him during the night and whether he might turn from a relatively harmless cadaver into a flesh-eating zombie. The result was a sleepless night spent tossing and turning and getting up to check on him. The truth is that he kept quiet, alternating reading and watching the Discovery Channel, and I could have saved myself the trouble. Still, better safe than maimed, as I always say.

I woke up the next morning, after the little sleep I had managed to get, to the sounds of slammed cupboard doors. Presently Joe was in my room, dressed up in my best suit, a checkered piece that had cost me an eyeball, beaming on me. It was weird how he seemed to be in a good mood, considering his situation. But then, I assume that he had to be in denial if he wanted to keep functioning. Still, that didn't give him the right to help himself to my wardrobe.

"What on earth are you doing, dressed up like that?" I asked.

"Lizzy is coming to take me to the museum," he said, and he sounded puzzled that I had to ask, "and of course I had to make myself decent."

"And what's that foul smell?" I asked, annoyed.

"It must be your after shave lotion, Dave. I'm afraid that I may have overdone it a bit, but, you know, I can't smell anything, and I couldn't tell if I'd used enough of it."

"You've used enough of it all right," I said, twitching my nose. He had probably used up all of it. But the bright side was that my lotion did a good job of covering his natural stench. "What time is it?" I asked. I didn't feel rested at all.

"Almost nine," he said. "And what do you plan to do about our investigation?"

So here he was, playing boss with me again, and I had to keep control of the situation.

"Plan?" I said, almost spitting out the word. "I have no plan. I don't know. I may be doing nothing at all. So what will you do," I asked, "whack me?"

"Whack *you*? What a strange notion. I would never whack you. You're my best friend."

I looked at him sideways. I had never heard him talk like that— I mean, expressing himself in a civil manner. His face, judging from whatever little expression it still had, showed that he was sincere. I felt relieved.

Lizzy arrived a few minutes later, and left with Joe. I didn't show my face until I heard that they were gone. I wasn't up to it. I dressed and left for the office, without drinking my usual cup of coffee. For some reason I didn't feel like drinking or eating in the apartment any more. The sweet stench of decay was all over the place and it reduced my stomach into knots. I might get some coffee and breakfast at the bar near my office later, but first I wanted to check my mail.

When I reached the cubbyhole I call my office, on the second floor of an old building that is home to a large colony of cockroaches, I knew immediately that something was wrong—the door was ajar, and I was quite sure that I had locked it going out the day before. It wasn't as if I kept anything of value in there, but one doesn't like to have strangers wandering uninvited into their office. I drew my gun from its shoulder holster and went in, gun first, kicking the door. Pimpled Fred was sitting at my desk. An anticlimax, but a welcome one. The anticlimax, I mean, not Fred who, in contrast, was entirely unwelcome.

Pimpled Fred and I went back a long way, to fifth grade in the same shabby school in the neighborhood where we both grew up. He had earned his nickname on account of a profusely pimpled face, which he still sported twenty-five years later. He owned the Blue Bird and six other joints, and had a hand in many lucrative rackets. In school he had already shown promise by shark-loaning to us, less business-oriented kids. I had hated him in school, and I hated him now.

"Get your ass off my chair," I said without lowering my gun. This business of goons appropriating my seats was starting to get on my nerves.

"I'm glad to see you too, Dave," said Fred with a twisted smile. "Why don't you take a seat and let me tell you to what you owe the pleasure of my visit?"

"'Cause I don't care, and if you're not out of that chair in under ten seconds, they'll have to bury you in it."

"OK, OK. No need to be touchy," said Fred, rising. He walked around my desk and seated himself in one of the worn-out armchairs reserved for my sporadic clients. I put the gun back in its holster, kicked the door closed, and sat behind my desk. I fixed my gaze on Pimpled Fred, and waited. I could see that he was fretful, but I wasn't going to make it easy for him to tell me why he was here.

"I hear you have taken an interest in Stupid Joe's death," he said at last.

So that was it. Giving that he owned the joint where someone had shot Stupid Joe, that made sense. And since I had been questioning the Blue Bird's manager, I knew he knew that I was somehow involved, but why waste a good opportunity to torment him?

"Who told you such a thing?" I asked.

"I hear things. You know I do."

"But why would that—assuming it were right, which I ain't saying it is—be any damn business of yours? You're not connected with the mob, as far as I know."

"No. But, you see, I've got a very delicate transaction going on right now, and this business of Joe's has come at the worst possible time. And then there is this broad that works for me at the Blue Bird, going around telling ghost stories about Stupid Joe turning up all alive with a hole in his chest the size of your head. And my informers tell me the police have lost Joe's body. I ask you, how can you lose a body the size of Joe's? I don't believe the police for a moment. They must be planning to use the theft of Stupid Joe's body for something. Maybe they are planning to raid a few places looking for it, and mine may be on the list. All this is very bad for business."

"Yeah, you can see how my heart is bleeding for you. It's all I can do to keep myself from crying. Well, it was nice of you to come and tell Uncle Dave about your troubles. I like you young people to come to me whenever you need comfort and advice. Now get the hell out of here. You're taking up space that I require for other purposes."

I wasn't interested in Pimpled Fred's troubles. I had enough with mine. All I wanted was for him to leave, but Fred apparently had other ideas. He frowned a bit—no doubt stung by my lack of sympathy—but didn't move.

"Look here," he said in a hoarse voice, "I need to know if this here that they tell me about you being involved is true or not. If it is,

I may have a proposition for you."

"What proposition?" I asked suspiciously.

"Assume for a moment—just for the sake of argument—that I knew who did Stupid Joe in. If I were to tell you, could you guarantee that you, and whoever is impersonating Joe's ghost, will stop sticking your noses into my business?"

"Assuming that I was sticking my nose into your business—which I am not—and assuming that I knew someone who was impersonating Joe's ghost—which is a stupid assumption to make anyways—then it would be reasonable to assume that I might be able to guarantee that neither I, nor this non-existing ghost impersonator, would keep sticking our respective noses into your business, *if* you were to tell us who did Stupid Joe in," I said, stopping to inhale before it was too late.

Pimpled Fred had been following my statement with a furrowed brow, leaning forward as if in an attempt to grasp its meaning.

"Do you mean to say 'Yes'?" he asked at last.

"Yes," I conceded.

"Then why don't you say so, damn you! Never mind. It was Tony Zuzzurello."

"Why would I believe you? Tony Zuzzurello is a little worm and I don't believe that he would have the nerve for doing something like that."

"I have it from the horse's mouth. Tony is seeing one of my girls and he bragged to her that he had done Joe in. Two minutes later she ran to tell me. And I happen to know—just in case you may wish to 'interview' him about it—that tonight he will be at home, all alone. The address is here," he added, handing me a slip of paper, which I folded and put into my wallet without looking at it.

"Ain't you gonna thank me?" he asked.

"For what? You haven't dropped dead yet, as far as I can tell."

"Ha, ha," he laughed lightly and reached for the door. "Remember our deal," he added, and was gone.

Tony Zuzzurello! That made a lot of sense. This Zuzzurello was a little rat of a hired hand who worked for Stupid Joe's family. The story, as I had heard it, was that one day, last year, he had incurred Joe's displeasure over a job not done well enough. Stupid Joe, I was told, had broken his fingers one by one, reciting all the while "This little piggy went to market." This couldn't have been pleasant for Tony Zuzzurello, and apparently he had decided to get even, big time. Well, now we had something to sink our teeth into. And if Pimpled Fred was right, we could wrap it up that night, and then I would get rid of Stupid Joe for good.

The good news worked wonders on my appetite and I went to my usual Chinese restaurant for pork chops and noodles. I was in a good mood and preparing to wrap myself around my meal, when a shadow fell on my table and a man in a felt hat seated himself uninvited before me. I knew who he was—one of the low-ranking members of Stupid Joe's family—all muscle and no brain. I waited for him to speak. He picked up an eggroll from my plate and ate it slowly without speaking. That's an old trick, meant to make you feel inferior and in awe of your visitor, which didn't really bother me.

"So, Dave," he said when he finished chewing, "is there anything you want us to tell me?"

"No," I said, and I went on eating as if he wasn't there.

That confounded him for a while and I could almost see wheels whirring in his head, trying to decide what to do next.

"The family is unhappy," he said at last.

"I'm sorry to hear that. Give them my condolences."

"That's not what I mean. The family is unhappy that you keep shoving your nose into its business. We know that you're going around asking questions about Joe Murray. That's not good. Questions attract attention and the family doesn't want attention."

"I can understand that."

"That's good, because I have a message for you. If you keep nosing around, you'll be sorry."

I didn't have a good repartee, so I just kept eating. He got up and leaned menacingly on the table.

"We'll be watching you," he said, and then he left.

It looked like everybody was competing to ruin my day. I finished my meal and drove back to the apartment.

But I wasn't through with intrusions, that day. Waiting for me on the mat was none other than Sergeant Wesley George, my eternal enemy. Well, in fact, we are not really enemies—I hate his guts and he can't stand me, but we cooperate from time to time, when it is worth our while. Right now, however, he was about the last person I wanted to see.

"You took your sweet time getting home," he complained.

I gazed at him scornfully. Where did this flatfoot get off telling me what to do, I wondered.

"Did you call my secretary about seeing me?" I asked, "Because you're not in my diary and I only see visitors by appointment."

"Cut the bull, Callaghan. Where is it?"

"Where is what?" I asked. I really didn't have a clue what he was talking about.

"Someone stole Stupid Joe's body from the morgue, and word on the street is that you are involved. So stop wasting my time and tell me where it is."

I made quite a production of searching my pockets, one by one, and then I turned to him.

"It ain't here. Sorry I can't help you," I said.

He didn't laugh.

"I've got a good mind to take you down to the station, and then we'll see if you still feel like wisecracking."

"Yeah? On what count? That some junkie on the street told you a fib to get you off his back? That would be a good one."

Boneheaded as he is, George knows when he's licked. He moved away from the door and started to walk away. He stopped after a few paces and threw over his shoulder, "This is not the last you've heard from me," and then he left.

Having the cops breathing down my neck was bad, especially since Joe was hanging out at my place and there was no telling if George would not come up with the bright idea of dropping by with a search warrant. Forget lying to the police; that would be the least of my worries. How would I explain keeping a pet zombie in my living room? I couldn't even start to think of an excuse.

CHAPTER 4

I had hoped to find Joe and break the news to him and luckily he was at home, again watching the Discovery Channel. He had become addicted to it and I had to switch off the TV to get his attention.

"Hey!" he complained. "I was watching that."

"No time for that," I rebuked him. "You already had your fun at the museum. How was it, by the way?"

"It was great. Huge. Elizabeth is a wonderful lady."

"Who?"

"Elizabeth. Lizzy."

"Yeah, Lizzy is a great gal. No doubt. I wouldn't call her 'a lady,' though."

Joe got up and looked at me with severity.

"Are you making disrespectful remarks about Elizabeth?" he asked menacingly.

"No, of course not," I said hastily. I was getting a glimpse of Stupid Joe, old style, and wasn't liking it.

"Because," he continued, making himself clearer, "I won't tolerate disrespect toward Elizabeth. She is the most divine creature I've ever met. She's kind, she's nice, and she teaches me a lot. Let me tell you this," he continued, and I could swear that his eyes, normally suggestive of those of a dead fish, had taken on a forceful light. "Mine has been a wasted life. Yes, entirely wasted. A complete washout. I've squandered my potential. But now, thanks to

Elizabeth, I have started my rehabilitation and I need to learn and improve. She's taking me to an open concert at City Gardens, tonight."

"Listen to me," I said, feeling that this was getting out of hand. "I hate to remind you of this, but you're dead. Your flesh is decaying, and soon you'll start leaving pieces of yourself around. You are in no position to start getting an education. OK? You must focus on our mission. Remember our mission? We have to find the one who did you in, do *him* in, and then it's *Requiescat in pacem* for poor Joe. You follow me?"

"You know," he rebuked me, "there's no need to get personal. You aren't that beautiful either. Are you aware of the fact that your front tooth is badly encapsulated? The effect is quite disagreeable. But do I tell you so? Of course I don't. My mommy taught me never to comment on other people's appearance. I wish you'd met my mommy," he added.

He spoke with a dreaming countenance that startled me, and I could swear that if alive, he would have shed a tear. He was obviously going bananas faster than I had thought and I had to bring him back to the practical issues before I lost his attention.

"Yes, yes. I'm sure she was charming. But now listen to me. I know who shot you. It was your old friend Tony Zuzzurello. And what's more, I know where he's gonna be tonight. Now you can go and whack him, and then you can return to your nice slab at the morgue. Isn't that great?"

Joe scratched his head and sat on the couch, peering pensively into the dark screen of the TV set.

"All of a sudden," he said, "I don't feel like whacking Tony Zuzzurello anymore. He's also a creature of God, you know. He also has a mother."

"He's nothing of the sort. He's a treacherous shooting-in-the-back son of unmarried parents and I don't think he has a mother. Besides, it was you who wanted to get even with him."

"I know, but ... Oh, I don't know. Perhaps we'll do it some other time. I promised Lizzy to go to the concert with her. She says that she can never talk you into going places—intellectual places, I mean—and I won't let her down. Now, if you'll excuse me, I need to get ready."

He got up and disappeared into my bathroom, to do what, God knew. I sat there in my armchair, feeling as if the roof had fallen on my head. If I had read the symptoms right, this walking piece of rotting meat was in love with my girlfriend. Can you beat that?

I don't know for how long I sat there, but when Joe came back my eyes met the most grotesque spectacle ever. Joe's face was red like that of an Indian chief in one of those old Hollywood movies, and the false beard was dangling from one cheek.

"What on earth have you put on your face?" I asked, amazed.

"It's make-up," he said. "Elizabeth happened to comment that I was a little pale, today—like a Greek god, I believe she said—and I thought that a bit of color was called for."

"You look like a painted doll. And the beard won't stick on all that powder. For God's sake, go and wash that muck off your face. Quick," I hurried him, as the doorbell rang, "this must be Lizzy."

Joe rushed back into the bathroom and I opened the door. It was Lizzy, as expected, and she walked in with a smile that immediately turned into an expression of disgust.

"Gosh, Dave, don't you *ever* open a window in here?"

In fact, I had opened all the windows, but it was of little use. I ushered her out quickly.

"I'm sorry. Problem with the drains. They'll fix it in a couple of days."

"Where is Gustave? We will be late for the concert."

"He's dressing. But wait a second. I need your help. I have a serious situation here." Lizzy is a good listener, so she simply opened her ears without asking silly questions, and I explained. "You see, J ... Gustave is not really a friend of mine. He's here for a job. A very important job. But as it turns out, he has got a crush on you ..."

"The precious little thing," she squealed.

"Yes, isn't it," I said with ill-concealed annoyance. "The fact is that right now his only interest is in you, and because of you he refuses to do his part and help me with the job. And if he doesn't, I'm in a fix. And I can't even begin to tell you how big a fix this is."

"Oh, I'm sorry. It's all my fault, isn't it? I've been too nice to him, but I couldn't help myself. He seems so helpless and polite. Doesn't he remind you of a fluffy teddy bear?"

"Don't be absurd!" I said, I couldn't help myself, and she looked hurt.

"Well, he does to me and you should respect that."

"Sure, I do," I said curtly. "But you must help me."

"How?"

"He'll do whatever you ask him to. You must tell him how much you value men who keep their word, and how distasteful you find those who go back on their promises. Tell him that you will never be able to be friends with a man who undertakes to do something, and then changes his mind. That will do the trick."

"That's simple. I can do it. No problem."

"Then do it. Do it now. I'll meet you after the concert—look for the Jaguar. And if you play your part right, he is sure to come with me and get the job done."

"Don't worry. I'm sure that he'll keep his word. He has such a delicate personality."

"Give me a break," I said, but this time I said it to myself.

Joe came out, looking much more normal than before, the

false beard now sticking in all the right places. I wished them an enjoyable evening and then I went back inside and invested a few minutes in the futile exercise of emptying two cans of air-freshener in my living room.

CHAPTER 5

I don't like to visit with Prof. Jonah. Years ago, when I started to see things, he convinced me that I was not off my rocker and sort of forced me to become who I am now. He's one of the few people who still give me the creeps, after all I've seen and done. On the other hand, he's also one of the few people who really know what to do when things get out of hand. So I went to see him.

But let me tell you about Prof. Jonah, before I go on telling my story. Perhaps half of what I know about the deadies I learned from him. The rest I learned busting my ass on assignments. At first, when I became a ghost-magnet, I don't mind telling you that I was spooked out of my wits. I didn't know what was going on and why dead people were seeking me out with weird requests. I remember the first time I saw one. I was a rookie detective then, working for a friend about whom I'll tell you some other time, and my assignment for the day was to stalk someone and see if he was stealing from his boss. He had gone into a building the other side of the street and I was standing smoking a quiet cigarette by a telephone booth, when suddenly this chick showed up out of nowhere.

"He's left by the back door," she said, giving me quite a jolt.

"Who the hell are you?" I asked.

At first I didn't realize that she was a ghost—she looked quite normal and I had never seen a ghost before—until she took a step forward and I saw through her. I almost pissed in my pants, I swear.

"Hell is right," she said, with a vicious smile on her face. "I'd like you to go and see Mike, and tell him he's a son of a bitch. Tell him I said so."

I barely managed to speak, but I had questions.

"Who's Mike, and who are you?" I asked, not unreasonably, I think.

"I, ahhh!" she said, and disappeared. Not a moment too soon, if you ask me.

I put that episode down to too much booze—I had heard that some of the less quality stuff could give you hallucinations—and that helped me to kept my sanity until the next time.

Less than a week after that hallucination, I had another one. This time someone knocked on my apartment door and when I went to see who it was, a man was already inside. He wore a raincoat and a hat, which was a damn silly thing to do in August when you wanted to strip off your skin to keep cool. He didn't look at me and seemed to have a particular interest in my rug.

"The cleaners haven't come yet," he said, in a low voice filled with exasperation. "Where are the cleaners?"

I had no idea who he was or what he was talking about and all I could do was stand there, listening to his complaints, until he turned around and walked out through the door. Well, healthy or not, I drank a good measure of scotch before my knees stopped shaking, and then I grabbed the telephone guide. Thumbing through it, I looked for psychic counsel, exorcists, and similar practitioners, until I ran into Prof. Jonah's ad. It ran like this:

Are you being persecuted by supernatural entities?

Are you tired of the old, ineffective exorcisms?

What if you could get control of your troubles and stop worrying about unfriendly manifestations?

Prof. Jonah's method has successfully rid hundreds of clients of bothersome apparitions.

Apply today! If you're not satisfied with the results, your money will be returned, no questions asked.

I was at the phone faster than you can say "supernatural apparition," and five minutes later I was on my way to meeting him. Prof. Jonah was and still is a lean, you could even say dried-up, sort of individual, with a beaky nose and bushy eyebrows. His manner is curt and unfriendly, but he knows all the ropes. I told him my trouble and he listened without interrupting. After a while, he got up and fetched a contraption that looked a cross between an Indian calumet pipe and a corkscrew, and fiddled with it around me for a while. Then he said, "Five hundred dollars".

"What do you mean, 'five hundred dollars'?" I asked.

"That's what it will cost you to hear my assessment of the problem."

I had no choice so I paid up.

"So, how do I stop seeing these people?"

"You don't," said Prof. Jonah, curtly.

"But I can't go on having those things showing up. It's draining me. I can't work, I can't sleep. I follow a subject and one of these ghosts pops up and scares me into losing him. You need to give me a cure. I paid for it."

"You paid to be given an honest assessment of the situation and here it is: you are a natural medium. You can't change that."

I argued, but it was hopeless. Then I tried adulation, and that too got me nowhere.

"Everybody says you're the best. You must be able to fix this for me," I said.

"Who's everybody? You never heard of me until one hour ago."

"Okay," I admitted, "but your ad still guarantees results, or money back."

"That's for a treatment. I'm not treating you, only assessing."

You get the idea. After a while, I stopped arguing and accepted the situation. Prof. Jonah agreed to teach me all I needed to get by in my new situation, for a hundred bucks a lesson. It was worth every cent, and that's why I keep going to him from time to time, when things get too hot for me to handle on my own.

I found him immersed in a book, as he is most of the time, but I suspect that he's just putting on an act for visitors.

"You're in trouble," he ruled before I even managed to open my mouth.

"In deep shit," I admitted.

"How do I know it?" he quizzed me.

"How do *I* know how you know it?" I retorted.

"Because I hear things and, besides, you never come to see me for pleasure. So what is it, this time?"

I gave him the picture. I was annoyed that he chuckled when I told him how Joe seemed to have fallen for Lizzy, but I knew by experience that he had to have all the facts, or else his advice might be useless. He heard everything, closed his eyes, leaned back and chewed on it for so long that I thought he might have died himself.

"An unstoppable," he said at last. "Quite special. I'm glad you told me about it. Scientifically speaking, this is extremely interesting."

"Yes, yes, I'm glad you're having fun with it, but what does it mean?"

"It means that the zombie is charged with practically unlimited energy and will go on until he is completely decayed, unless ..."

"Yes?" I said. "Keep that 'unless' going. That's what I came here for."

The old man likes to be theatrical, so he waited just long enough to get on my nerves before going on.

"To stop an unstoppable you need to bring him back to the place where he got the energy he's using, so he can return it to its source. As simple as that."

"The morgue!"

"If his story is right, the morgue, indeed."

"I knew it! He promised to go back to the morgue, but now he's changed his mind. What can I do?"

"A hundred dollars, please," the old thief said.

"Again? I already paid you more than a thousand."

"That was ages ago and it was for your education, not to solve a case."

I paid the old vulture, silently wishing that he would choke on it.

"So what's the solution?" I said, after he pocketed the money.

"You must convince him to go back to the morgue."

"I already knew that," I said, "but how?"

"Ah, I have no suggestions. Use your talent and imagination," he said, without blushing.

I could have forced him to give me back my money, but I didn't. Sometimes Prof. Jonah comes in handy and I have to let him steal a little from me, from time to time. That's maintenance money. Nevertheless, I left without saying goodbye, and I meant it to sting.

CHAPTER 6

"Lizzy!" I called when I saw her coming toward me in the crowd, with Stupid Joe wobbling at her side. His walk had deteriorated noticeably during the last twenty-four hours, and he was barely able to keep up with her.

"Hi, kids," I greeted them when they reached me. I was standing with my back to the Jaguar, which I had parked at the curb.

"What are you doing here?" asked Joe. His manner was unfriendly and suspicious, and I didn't like it.

"I'm here to remind you that you gave me your word of honor..."

"About what?" he asked, as if trying to remember.

"You said that you would go back to where you belong—you know what I'm talking about—as soon as we finished running this small errand we have on our agenda. Remember?"

"Yes, yes, but I can't be bothered now. Elizabeth and I have plans."

"But you know that I'm counting on you to get the job done and that I can't do it without your help. Besides, you promised," I said, looking desperately at Lizzy.

"Did you now, Gustave?" she asked, gazing at him wide-eyed. These chicks can act so innocent while they twist you around their little finger, that sometimes I wonder if they're not putting on an act all the time.

"Well ... mm ... I guess I did—but that was before I met you.

It's a whole new situation now."

"You know, Gustave, that I have ideals and I am demanding of people whom I can call my friends."

She smiled sweetly and made it sound ominous at the same time.

"What do you mean by 'demanding'?" Joe asked, seeming confused.

"I expect the highest ethical standards of my friends."

That was too much for a stupid mobster to digest and he had clearly lost her, so I butted in and translated.

"What she means is that if you don't play it straight you won't be in her league and she'll cut you." I explained.

Lizzy nodded in agreement and I thought that Joe's shoulders sagged a bit.

"You understand how I feel about keeping one's word, I hope, Gustave," she added, and at the right moment too. Joe was starting to realize that he was in a fix and we needed to hammer it home.

"Yes, but this is really nothing. Dave here won't mind if we skipped our little errand this time, would you, Dave?" he asked, sounding hopeful.

I wasn't going to bail him out, of course. "In fact, I would mind it very much," I said. "Get in the car, please," I added, opening the door for him.

Joe's gaze went from me to Lizzy and back a couple of times, searching for a way out, but Lizzy's expression didn't leave anything to the imagination, bless her soul, and Joe had no choice but to give up.

"OK, but then I drive," he said, showing me the his hand.

Resigned, I dropped my car keys into his hand, and sat in the passenger seat. Joe got in, waved goodbye to Lizzy, started the engine and drove off with a strident sound of burnt tires. Showing off, that's what I call it.

Miraculously, we managed to reach Tony Zuzzurello's address without crashing into anything. We stopped near the house and Joe cut the engine.

"What now?" he asked.

"Simple. We go in, grab Tony, you get even with him, and we leave. Any questions?"

"You know," said Joe, looking embarrassed, "I don't really feel as if I cared any more. Why don't we forget about Tony Zuzzurello and go see a good movie instead?"

"Because that is not what we have agreed upon. I agreed to find the one who did you in, and you agreed to get back to the morgue as soon as you are through taking care of him. So now you're going to get even with Tony, and you're going to like it."

"All right. But perhaps all I need to do is to scare the hell out of him. I'll reveal myself to him. That should do the trick."

I considered it. "Will you feel that you have gotten even afterwards?" I inquired.

"More than even. Absolutely ahead of the game."

"Then I don't object," I said. And I didn't. One corpse less to account for was all for the best, particularly since it might be difficult to sell the police on the idea that Stupid Joe had done him in.

We got out of the car and walked toward the house. A little light was coming from what I assumed was the living room. I decided that pushing the bell was as good an approach as any, so that's what I did.

"Who's there?" asked a voice from within.

"Electricity inspector, sir," I answered in my best respectable tone. "We have a short circuit in the transformer down the street, and we need to check that your fuses are in order, because of fire hazards."

You wouldn't believe it, but Tony Zuzzurello was dumb enough to bite, and opened the door. Perhaps he didn't know what a transformer was, or he was nervous about fires. Still, I hadn't expected it to be so easy and to some extent I was disappointed. The moment I saw the crack of an inch I pushed the door with all my weight, which is considerable, and Tony went flying down the corridor. Joe and I walked in, keeping an eye on the little rat on the floor.

"May we come in?" I asked with my most frightening smirk after I finished locking and bolting the door. We didn't want to be disturbed.

"Who ... who? What do you want?" asked Tony with an equal mixture of fear and confusion.

"We want you, Tony," said Joe with that rasping voice that I had learned to tolerate, but which I understood was scary when you heard it for the first time.

"Who are you?" whined Tony. He was still sitting on the ground, his back to the wall, and was making a pathetic attempt to inch away from us.

"I'm your nemesis," said Joe, and once again I was amazed to discover that he had learned words such as "nemesis." It occurred to me that, to some extent, it seemed that he had indeed improved his education.

"My what?" asked Tony, missing the point entirely.

"I'm Joe Murray," thundered Joe.

"Impossible," was Tony's reaction. "I know that I have ... that poor Joe has been shot and is dead. You can't fool me."

"Yeah?" I threw at him. "Then where is Joe's body?"

"I have no idea. I don't have it here, I can tell you that."

"Yes you do!" thundered Joe, ripping off his beard.

I couldn't help admiring the dramatic effect he achieved. Tony opened his mouth, then closed it and finally opened it again. It seemed as if it would stay open for good. He covered his eyes with both hands, and started whimpering and shaking his head vigorously from side to side.

Joe drew his pistol and pointed it at Tony. He kept it there for a full minute, but Tony wasn't paying any attention. Eventually Joe pocketed his gun and turned around, leaving Tony Zuzzurello to perform creative contortions on the floor. I ran after him, relieved.

"Does this mean that we are done here?" I inquired.

"Yup. He's got a nasty shock, don't you think?"

I looked at Joe's face. It showed the nearest thing to a smile that I had ever seen on him.

"He'll probably stay on the floor for a day or two. Are you satisfied now? No more revenge needed?"

"Nah! That's enough. Hey!" he called out with excitement, looking at a small table near the door, "these are the keys to Tony's Mercedes."

Joe pocketed the keys and walked out. Tony's Mercedes was parked outside and he unlocked the door and sat behind the wheel. I leaned forward and looked at him. He behaved like a child who had just been given a big toy. He was playing with all the buttons on the dashboard and turning switches on and off.

"Do you think that Elizabeth would like this car?" he asked after a while.

"I guess so. Nothing wrong with a Mercedes," I said. No harm in being accommodating, now that he was going away for good.

Joe looked pensive—at least, as much as his inexpressive face permitted—and he was obviously going through some emotions, now that the show was at an end.

I was sorry for him, rotting away at a young age, and I felt mild regret, mixed with relief, that our ways were parting. After a while, I cleared my throat to get his attention.

"Yes? What?" he asked, tearing himself away from the gadgets on the dashboard.

"I understand that you'll be going back to your slab at the morgue in Tony's Mercedes. Good choice. Elegant way to go. Well, it was nice having you with us, and I wish you all the best. If that's all right with you, I'll be going now."

Joe attempted an appreciative smile, actually making an awful smirk, and nodded, pulling the door closed. I stepped back, waiting for the Mercedes to move, but Joe lowered his window and looked at me.

"I wanted to thank you for all your help, Dave. I really appreciate it. Well," he added, starting to drive away, "I'll be seeing you."

Poor Joe. I looked at him, fumbling at the wheel with hands that refused to function properly. It was pathetic. The car jumped forward in a series of hiccups and then stopped, drove back to me in reverse, and Joe opened his window again. He looked at me with an expression that was the closest thing to a smile I had ever seen on him.

"Oh, and Dave," he said, speaking over the noise of the engine, "don't wait up for me tonight. I have a key."

Then the car slid away into the night

EPISODE TWO

PHANTOM LOVER

CHAPTER 1

It was bad enough, I can assure you, finding a half-naked ectoplasm sitting at my desk, but she had to talk nonsense too. Wait a second. What I mean is, there was a woman sitting there, but she wasn't a real, live woman—she was a spirit manifesting out of ectoplasm. I had barely managed to collect my wits after the initial shock of finding her there, when I walked into my office, and she whispered urgently, "Here she comes! Not a word to her!", made a whooshing sound, and pumped herself into an open drawer in my filing cabinet.

I wasn't given time to ponder over her strange behavior, because right then someone knocked on my door and the silhouette on the glass panel told me that I had a female visitor. I pushed the drawer closed and considered my options. I could ignore the visitor, and she would probably give up after knocking on the door for a while without response. On the other hand, I don't get that many potential clients coming to see me, and chasing a potentially paying client away was against my principles. There was of course a danger that if I let her in the ectoplasm might jump up from the cabinet drawer and give her a heart attack, but she had seemed anxious to avoid meeting my visitor so I assumed that she'd rather stay put in that closed drawer.

Another timid knock on the door tipped the scale. My visitors usually knock once and then start kicking the door if I don't open immediately. A polite one was a refreshing experience and worth meeting.

"Mister Callaghan ..." she said as I opened the door.

"Yes?" was my curt answer. I know I wasn't being inviting, but it was a miracle that I could speak at all since all the commotion was starting to get to me; my mouth was dry and my tongue seemed to be in the process of swelling up to twice its normal size.

I took a good look at her. She was young—no more than thirty years old—good looking and polite. Not the kind you would expect to see in my neighborhood. Something was obviously weighing on her mind. Her gaze was fixed on the floor, and it looked like she would stand on the mat forever, unless I did something about it.

"Are you going to stand there much longer?" I finally managed to say. I added an inviting smile to make up for my earlier curtness.

She hesitated, and I wondered if she would ever speak. "I'm sorry for coming unannounced," she said at last, smiling a timid smile, "but I need your help. May I come in?"

I nodded and moved aside, closing the door behind her. I circled around her and took position in the chair recently vacated by the ectoplasm. My visitor sat in the battered one before my desk; she watched me anxiously and kept twisting her hands nervously. I barely noticed her nervousness though. I was too busy gaping at her. I had never had such a classy customer in the rat hole that I call my office, and I was having a hard time believing that she was actually there to hire me. At last, she looked me straight in the eyes and spoke.

"You see, Mister Callaghan ..." she started to say.

That was a way of starting our acquaintance on the wrong foot.

You can never develop a real relation with people who mister you. "Dave," I corrected her. "Please call me Dave; that's what everybody calls me."

"Mister ... Dave," she said hesitantly, "I don't know how to tell you this."

"Well," I said as politely as I could manage, "then we are in a bit of a fix, aren't we? I can hardly help you if I don't know what your problem is. Why don't you start by telling me how you got here and what kind of help you need?"

I really wished that she would get on with it and let me go back to the main business of the day—finding out who that ectoplasm was and what she wanted from me. I sat in my chair with my right leg reaching out to hide the carcass of a large winged cockroach with my shoe. I had been meaning to kick it out of there for days, but kept putting it off. I hoped that she hadn't noticed it.

"I ... I really need your help, Mister ... Dave." She was wearing a white overcoat over a white dress, with what could have easily been a string of small real diamonds worn around her neck. I hoped it wasn't, though, because walking around in my neighborhood with that kind of ice out in the open was inviting trouble. Her hat, also white, had a feather stuck in it. She looked like an angel. More importantly, she oozed wealth.

"I'm listening," I said invitingly.

"My husband—we've been married for two years now—is having an affair. Oh!" she exclaimed, "this is so difficult ..."

The guy must be crazy, I thought. This gal looked like a million dollars and they had been married for only two years. What's wrong with these rich people? Quite a jerk he must be. I waited for her to go on speaking. She seemed to have trouble collecting her thoughts, and I decided that rushing her wouldn't help, so I limited my reaction to a few sympathetic noises. After a minute, she continued.

"Mister Zapowski told me that you are the only detective who can handle this for me," she said at last.

"Wait a minute," I said. This needed some careful consideration and I needed a moment to think. Al Zapowski specialized in divorce cases. There was nothing that he liked more than taking pictures of cheating husbands. He had a whole collection of them and once said to me that he was going to sell them and retire on the proceeds. We were colleagues, but not pals, and giving up a client to me wasn't in character, so there had to be strings attached.

"Zapowski handles this type of case exclusively, so why isn't he working on it for you?" I asked. Knowing Zapowski for a low individual as I did, I was fully justified to be suspicious.

"He did, at least for a while, until he realized what was happening. Perhaps I should tell you this from the beginning."

"That would be a good place to start," I agreed.

"A few weeks ago I started to feel that something was wrong with my husband. He had started to come home late, to go out at all times and to stay in bed for days. I engaged Zapowski's services to find out what was going on. By then I had a strong suspicion that he was having an affair. Zapowski followed my husband and witnessed one of his amorous encounters. That was when he told me that I should come to you."

"I still don't get it," I said.

"He said ... he said that you have experience with the

supernatural. You see, the woman that my husband is seeing ... she's a ghost."

"Pardon me?" I said. She had gotten my attention there.

"Oh, I don't know what the technical word is—maybe an ectoplasm or something—but that's the essence of the problem. She has put some sort of spell on him, and is sucking all his life out of him. Look at this," she said. She stood up and handed me a photograph. "This is my husband six months ago."

I studied the picture. The man in it was sort of plump, with eyes that reminded me of a dead halibut I had seen on a fishermonger's slab recently. He was richly dressed, but the sight failed to bring about the elation that my client seemed to expect me to feel.

"And this is a picture of him that Mister Zapowski took last week," she added, handing me a large print. The man in it bore only a vague resemblance to the one in the first picture. He was emaciated, his suit was too large for him and it hung on him as it would on a coat-hanger; his back was slightly bent and he looked much older than in the first picture. "You see what I mean?" she asked vehemently. She got up and began pacing the room nervously.

"Sit down, Mrs. ... ?" I said dryly.

"Wermeyer. Emma Wermeyer. And my husband is—"

"Otto Wermeyer," I said quickly. I knew who they were—rich, influential, the last people you would expect to find getting into trouble.

"Yes," she murmured modestly, as if being famous and rich was something for which she needed to apologize. She sat down again and lowered her gaze to the floor.

I looked at Emma Wermeyer, this time weighing her up carefully. If she was to become my client, I had to get to know her well. She was quite easy on the eye and looking her over wasn't an ordeal. I did so four or five times, until she blushed and then I reverted to my best business manners.

"Okay, Mrs. Wermeyer. If you want me to take the case I'll need a few hard facts from you first, and a retainer."

She took out her checkbook and scribbled quickly in it. When she was done writing, she tore a check from the book and handed it over to me. "Is that enough?" she asked.

It was enough to buy her my undivided attention for the next year, so I folded it carefully and put it in the inner pocket of my jacket, and then I switched on my best smile and looked her straight in the eyes.

"That'll do, for the time being," I said. "Let's have the details."

As soon as the door closed behind Emma Wermeyer, a rattling sound came from the drawer of the file cabinet that my ectoplasm had selected for her hideout, and here she was again, slumped in my chair like she owned the place. She actually looked quite nice, with a tiny red dress that only pretended to cover her generous breasts and curves. I did wish she would stop flickering, though, and the fluid, ever-changing shape of her body was an antidote to concentration.

"Who *are* you?" I managed to say at last.

"I'm Daphne, nice to meet you, Dave," she answered, making it sound like a casual social encounter.

"Forget nice!" I barked. "Not nice. Not nice at all! What are you doing here? What do you want?"

"You heard that ... that slanderous bitch. She's ruining my business with her—what do you call those? Baseless allegations?"

"That's legalese. I'm not a lawyer," I said in despair. I sat in the client's chair and took my head in my hands. "Please, please, explain so it makes some sense," I pleaded.

"All right. But you're the private eye with supernatural experience, right? Everybody says you're the only one."

I nodded, too tired to ask who "everybody" was, and she continued.

"Look here. I know I'm not a lady like that bitch who just left; I'm a hooker, true, but that's the only way I can make an honest life ... death, I mean. I take some vital juice from my clients in return for my services, but just enough to keep me going. It's nothing to the client—less than giving a little blood—and they never mind. Did you ever donate blood, Dave?"

"Yes, yes, I did. What has that to do with all this?"

"Nothing. It's just to give you an idea of how it is. You don't even notice it after a few minutes. That's what happens when I take payment. I would never take more from a client than I needed. It would be unprofessional and, besides, it would wear a potentially good client out. So the way I do it, it's a good bargain. And I'm well worth it ... want me to show you?" she asked invitingly.

She made a wavy movement toward me, as if ready to show me how worthy she was, but stopped when I raised my hand, palm forward.

"Under other circumstances I would love to," I lied, "but it's a professional rule I stick to, never to mix work and pleasure. Perhaps some other time," I added.

"Sure," she said without blinking. "Any time. Just say the word. Anyways, I'm not the one who's sucking that sucker dry. I'm being framed and you're going to help me find out who's doing it."

I raised my head and gazed at her. I had a few simple questions that I had to get out of my system.

"Why do you care who's doing it, if you're not involved? That's fishy, if you ask me. And why do *I* care? And why do you think I'd lift my little finger for you? Answer me that," I threw at her.

She remained unruffled and said, "I care because all this gossip about drying the customers up is scaring them away, and if I have no customers I get no juice and, puff! There goes good old Daphne. And you care because you're being paid by the rich bitch to do just that, and you might as well do it right. And when this is over I'll make it worth your while to have been nice to poor, little Daphne. It's a promise."

"You owe me nothing," I hastened to say. "As you said, I'm paid to do a job." She had a point, I had to hand that to her. And she was a straight talker, in a way that I found disarming. In any case, there was no harm in getting information from her. "Tell me all you know," I said, pulling out my notebook. I rarely write anything in it, and I keep it mostly to impress people that I am questioning, but my head was a beehive and if ever there was a time that I needed to take notes, that was that time.

Emma Wermeyer had spoken for twenty minutes and Daphne for another half hour, but all I got out of their chatter was a headache.

I needed some place to start, though, and Daphne was as good a starting point as any.

"Since you say that it's not you, sucking Wermeyer dry—and I believe you," I hastened to say when I saw her expression changing into one of offense, "we must assume that he's seeing a colleague of yours, so I'll have to talk to some of your kind," I said. "Where can I find them?"

"Everybody has her favorite place, but we change places after a while, so I wouldn't know for sure. Your best bet is to try the fisherman's wharf first."

"And once I get there, how do I find them? And how do I talk them into cooperating?"

"I don't know. You're the detective. Find a way."

I pocketed my notebook and gazed at Daphne, undecided about what to do next.

"You haven't given me any useful leads, you know?" I said. In fact, I had taken down a couple of points that were worth checking, but I didn't want her to get above herself and think that she was really helping.

"Well, that's what I can think of. What do you want me to do now?"

"Get lost."

"You're rude, you know? Don't you want to know how to find me if you need me?"

"I won't be needing you. Not more than a pain in the neck I won't."

She was clearly enraged and didn't mince her words.

"You're a son of a bitch!" she almost shouted. "You're a—" she added, and puff she went, disappearing into thin air. I had counted on her doing just that. I've had ectoplasms doing the very same thing before. When you are an ectoplasm, you shouldn't get too excited or you are bound to find yourself thrown all the way from New York to Bombay. I chuckled at the thought of how easily I had tricked her into disappearing. I *am* good, damn good! At last, I was free to get down to business without having uninvited ghosts breathe down my neck.

CHAPTER 2

This business of life-sucking whores was new to me, and people will tell you that I'm a thorough bastard who does his homework on a case, which I am. I needed to understand much better how the racket worked, before I started to dig into the problem. With the fat retainer that I got from Emma Wermeyer, I had no qualms hiring some help to do research, but first I had to cash that check. The cashier at the bank lifted an eyebrow an eighth of an inch after reading the sum written on it but, after demanding to see two photo IDs to make sure that I was real, he paid up like a gentleman.

My next stop was at a joint on Third Avenue, where I hoped to find someone I knew. He wasn't there, but I wasn't entirely out of luck. In a booth, making love to a glass of beer, I saw Carl the Nose, called that because of the huge beak he sports in the middle of his face. Carl is good at nothing, really, except perhaps at petty thefts, but has got it into his fat head that he was born to be a private eye like me. He pleaded with me for ages to take him on as a trainee and was so insistent that I had made a habit of avoiding him. This time, instead, I walked straight to him.

"Hi Carl," I said, and he looked up, an expression of surprise all over the small portion of his face that was not covered by his nose.

"Oh, hi!" he said, getting up politely.

"Sit down," I said bluntly (I hate it when people start to act all reverent to me) and sliding my butt on the seat before him. "I have a job for you."

"A house or an office?"

"Not that kind of job. A real investigation job."

"No kiddin'?"

"No. It's a real one. But it's very delicate ... hmm, perhaps on second thought you're not cut out for it."

"Yes I am. I am too!"

"It involves women. How are you with women?"

That was when, as expected, Carl embarked on a long explanation of his experience with women, much of it made up from reading cheap magazines. I let him ramble on for a while. When he was over telling me about his prowess with the gentle sex, I explained his assignment to him. By then, he was too invested in his image as a womanizer to bail out.

"Let me see if I got this straight," he said. He was a little pale and stammered a bit, but kept a straight face. "You want me to go to the pier, find a whore, but not a regular one, and question her?'

"That's the idea," I confirmed.

"And this woman is a poltergeist, you say?"

"The technical term is 'ectoplasmic hooker'. That's a sexy hooker made of ectoplasm. A poltergeist has no consistence."

"I'll be damned!"

"I don't think that it'll go as far as that."

"But why would she talk to me?"

"I'll explain again," I said patiently. "This, as I said, is an undercover job. You'll go there as a client. You need to develop a relationship with her, and then she'll talk to you. You need to find out which hooker has Otto Wermeyer as a regular client, where she sees her clients, and anything else that you can learn."

"How do I do that?"

"You tell her that you are a friend of Otto's, that he keeps telling you about the wonderful experience he is having, but he's jealous and refuses to tell you where he goes for it. He got you so excited about it that you must find the hooker he sees and try her too."

"And I don't need to pay her?"

"Nope. These two hundred dollars that I'm giving you for the job stay in your pocket. She'll take another form of payment. You'll be giving her a little of your energy."

"How much should I give her?"

"She'll take what she needs. Just a little. You won't even notice it. Let's get going," I added, getting up. I didn't want to give him the time to start brooding on it.

It was getting late. I had been waiting for Carl to come back for two hours now, and I couldn't imagine what was keeping him. We had agreed to meet at the closer end of the fisherman's wharf and I had taken position there beside a ruined warehouse. The air was thick with the smell of fish and of decay, and the silence, broken every now and then by startling sounds, was beginning to make me edgy. Finally, I could wait no longer and decided to take a walk along the wharf and see if I could find him.

The atmosphere was definitely eerie. Long shadows, cast by a few dispersed lights, changed shapes as I walked, and the air was getting colder with every step—or perhaps that was just my imagination. As I walked past a pile of garbage a sound broke the silence.

"Ahhh!" it went. It was a kind of satisfied "Ahhh," not someone crying in pain.

I turned around and inspected the garbage more closely. The top layer was no ordinary garbage—it was Carl. He gazed at me with semi-closed eyes and had an idiotically ecstatic expression on his face.

"Carl! What's the matter with you?"

"Hilda. Amazing Hilda. Listen to me, Dave, she's amazing," he mumbled, smiling a vapid smile.

"Sit up!" I ordered, pulling his hand. He sat on the garbage, placed his fists under his chin, and gazed at me with watery eyes.

"I must tell you, Dave, nothing like this ever happened to me. She's awesome."

"Yes, I'm glad you enjoyed yourself. Now tell me what you learned from her."

"Oho! You want the juicy details, ah? The things she knows—"

"I don't care about that," I interrupted him. "You were supposed to question her and to bring back the information I asked for. Give it to me."

"Information?" Carl furrowed his brow as if the notion sounded completely new to him. "Like what?"

"Like what she knows about Otto Wermeyer and who he's seeing."

"Who's Otto Wermeyer?" Carl asked, as if hearing this name for the first time.

"Focus, dammit! Otto Wermeyer is the subject, the one I sent you to investigate about. You can't have forgotten him."

Carl smiled a crooked smile and gazed straight into my face.

"I'll tell you, Dave, Hilda can make you forget anything. Anything. You should try it some time. At first she said that she was giving me only a half hour, but then I asked for more and she agreed. And then some more—I can't remember how many sets we had— and then I think I passed out for a while. But it was worth it, believe me."

"Did you ask her about Otto Wermeyer or not?"

Carl's face took on an offended expression. He lay down again on the pile of garbage and curled up into a fetal position.

"How dare you ask me a question like that? I'm offended. Yes, deeply offended. Go away, Dave," he said. "I will die now."

He then started to snore through his gigantic nose. There was no point in trying to get any more from him, so I left him to his garbage and walked away.

CHAPTER 3

I had to start earning my retainer somehow, so I decided to talk to Zapowski. I finally tracked him down, sitting in a sordid bar behind the fish pier. He wasn't happy to see me, which was strange since he had recommended me to the client.

"Wha'd'ya want?" he asked curtly.

"Information," I said, simply.

"Ain't got none," he mumbled.

I looked at him. His fat belly bulged from under a dirty shirt and his gray jacket looked the worse for wear. He directed his gaze above my shoulder, a clear sign that he was lying to me.

"You should change your shirt more often, Al. It had that egg spot on it last time I met you, two months ago."

"Get out of my face, Dave. You're blocking my view of the Subject." He sounded genuinely pissed, but I wasn't buying it.

"Who's your subject?"

"Yeah, like I'm gonna tell you," he said dismissively.

"Okay, then tell me why you sent the Wermeyer woman to me."

"I was doing you a favor, you asshole. It's called 'referral' and it's done among colleagues, you know?"

"I'm gonna kiss you in a moment, Al. But before I do that you're going to take me to that hooker and show me where Otto

Wermeyer meets her."

"Says who?" Zapowski asked scornfully. I could see the derision in his porcine eyes.

"Says this little sister," I answered, pushing the muzzle of my .38 into his thick, fat neck. I was in no mood for niceties.

"Are you out of your mind, Dave?" Zapowski's expression turned serious, and I knew I had gotten through to him.

"Nope, just in a hurry. Get up!"

I should have known that something was wrong when Zapowski came docilely with me and only cursed me at odd spots. It was all too easy. The three-story building where Otto Wermeyer's phantom lover conducted her business in Chinatown, stood next to the backdoor to a Chinese restaurant. We took position behind a dumpster that smelled worse than Zapowski and only had to wait for half an hour, during which he became lyrical about my parents, particularly my mother, before Otto Wermeyer showed up. I compared him with the recent photograph that Emma had given me and it was unmistakably him. I watched as he walked through the narrow entrance.

"Happy now?" Zapowski said, acidly. "Now go and fuck yourself; I'm done with you."

I had no more use for him, so I waved him away with the .38 and he hastened to leave, still hissing profanities, until his voice was lost in the distance. Light appeared in a second-floor window and I watched as Wermeyer closed the blinds. Then I heard unmistakable noises meaning that someone was making a customer very happy the other side of those blinds.

"See, it's not me," a disembodied voice spoke in my ear, which made me bite my tongue and almost jump into the dumpster.

"You again!" I almost yelled in exasperation. "What are you doing here?" I asked, after the haze coming from the garbage bin next to me changed shape and revealed itself as Daphne.

"I'm here to help," she said, defensively.

"Well, you're not helping. Not a bit," I retorted.

"If you don't want me to help, I won't. But I thought you might like to know that there is no ectoplasm in that room."

"How do you know?" I asked. A stupid question, I guess.

"Really ..." she answered, rather disdainfully.

"Oh, all right. You could be useful," I conceded, "but you're wrong. I've seen Wermeyer go in and from what I hear he's having a good time."

"I'm not wrong. If he's having a good time it's with a living hooker, not with one of us."

That gave me some food for thought. If Daphne was right— and chances were that she was—our friend Otto was naughtier than his wife realized. I debated for a moment what to do. Spying on regular cheating husbands is a sleazy job and not really what I like to do, but I had to bring some real evidence back to Emma, to make her realize that Zapowski had screwed up and that her husband was seeing a regular hooker, not a ghostly one. To do that, I had to go up and take a picture to bring back to her. With a sigh, I took my camera from the pocket of my raincoat, but before I managed to turn it on all hell broke loose. Sirens came from everywhere and three police cars stopped just in front of the building, with screeching sounds of burning tires. Policemen jumped out of the car, guns in hands, and I realized that the prudent thing was to get the hell away from that place. I didn't know what they were after, but whatever it was I wanted no part of it. Still, I needed to know if Wermeyer was involved so I ignored common sense and my better instinct that was telling me to run, and instead I waited behind the dumpster. Daphne had disappeared without saying a word. She had this annoying habit of appearing and disappearing without warning, but after a while she came back.

"Why are you still here?" she asked.

"I'm waiting to see what the police are doing. If they leave I may still want to go up and surprise Wermeyer."

"You do know that this building has a back exit, right? Wermeyer is gone. He ran so fast that he must be ten miles away by now."

"Damn!"

"Damn is right. And the police will be staying around for a while. They got a tip and found a drug dealer with a nice supply on the first floor. This is a lovely neighborhood," she added with a smile.

"Tell me, was anybody with Wermeyer when he ran away?"

"No, he was all alone."

"So where was the hooker he was meeting?"

"Search me. I didn't see anybody else."

"Which means that you were wrong and he was seeing one of your kind. A regular hooker cannot disappear into thin air."

"I can't explain it, but I'm sure I wasn't wrong. Something's very weird here."

"Weird, ah? You don't say."

"What do we do now?" she asked.

"I don't know about you. I'm going home to take a shower and do some thinking."

"May I come with you?"

I considered it. I was at a loose end and she couldn't make it any worse. In fact, she might be useful, the way she went places without having to bother using keys.

"As you wish. Tag along, if you like."

I walked away. I was in a foul mood and it was all for the best that Daphne kept her mouth shut all the way.

CHAPTER 4

I live in a cozy bachelor apartment that I try to keep tidy. I opened the door, hung my raincoat and hat and sank into my armchair, in which I remained seated for a couple of minutes before getting up to fix myself a drink. All the while, Daphne stood at the window, gazing out, and I did my best to ignore her, until she spoke.

"We're fucked," she said.

"Aren't we," I agreed. I poured a good measure of scotch in my glass and then I picked up the phone. "Let me make a phone call."

I had a sudden hunch that I needed to check out. Every now and then I do favors for people in the force—it's good practice to cultivate some pals there. Not a long time ago, I had helped out someone in Narcotics with a big problem he had with a girlfriend that he really didn't want his wife to know about. I dialed his number.

"Hello, it's me," I said, when he answered.

"Oh, hi. It's been a while. What's up?"

"I need some information that I hope you can give me."

"Try me."

"A little over one hour ago there was a big operation in a building in Chinatown. Some of your people were there, and I heard that the target was a drug dealer."

"You're right. It was a big bust. The guys here are all bragging about it. What is it to you?"

"In itself, nothing at all, but I heard that you got tipped about it and I need to know where the tip came from."

"I shouldn't be telling you this," said my pal, lowering his voice, "it's against orders, but I'll tell you if you swear to keep it to yourself."

"Of course."

"The tip came from a private investigator. A friend of the chief."

"Was it Al Zapowski?" I asked. A telling silence followed at the other end of the line.

"Officially, I don't know."

"And unofficially?"

There was another silence on the line. It went on for so long that I started to think that he had hung up on me, but then he spoke again.

"I don't know how you know it, but unofficially, it is him. That's what I heard, but if the chief hears that I confirmed it, he'll skin me alive."

"Don't worry, he won't," I promised, and after a few words of thanks I hung up.

My hunch was correct. I don't believe in coincidences and the police raid, coming a short time after Zapowski had left, which had got in the way of my investigation, was too much of a coincidence for me to swallow. Now I had to figure out what was Zapowski's game. He obviously was deep in all this, but as to what "this" was, I was clueless.

"I'm going to take a shower," I said to the room.

In the shower, I turned on the hot water and let it run to make some steam, then I undressed. I was just about to go under the water jet when Daphne materialized in the middle of the room.

"What the hell are you doing here?" I yelled. I covered myself instinctively. I am not shy as a rule, but I mean, there is a limit to the shit I'll take, even from the deadies.

"Chill out," she said, unfazed. "Nothing of what you have there is new to me—and, by the way, you look good. I just got an idea and wanted to tell you about it."

"Well, get the hell out of here and tell me after I have my shower. I need it to be able to think."

"May I watch while you shower?"

"Scram!" I yelled.

"Oh, all right. No need to get testy. I'm leaving, but you're passing on a good thing. I could make the shower a lot more interesting for you."

I said nothing and after a few seconds she got the message and dissolved away.

The shower really invigorated me. I dressed up in shorts and a T-shirt and then I went to the kitchen to fix myself something to eat. Of course, Daphne was there, omnipresent as always.

"Good shower?" she asked.

I ignored her. She was getting way too familiar, and I had to watch it. You should never let a ghost become too close to you, no matter what form it is taking.

A baloney sandwich and a beer were what the doctor ordered and, followed by strong coffee, made me feel fit for thinking again.

"I need some more information, if I want to crack this one," I said. "I'll go and talk to Emma again."

"I'm coming with you."

"No, you're not. You stay put, or go to work, or whatever, but don't get near Emma Wermeyer or you and I are done."

"All right. No need to threaten me. I'll wait for you here."

"Good," I said, and left.

As I pushed the bell at the gate of Emma's house, I wasn't sure how much I would tell her. Women always talk too much, and I had no reason to believe that Emma was an exception. I couldn't count on her to keep her mouth shut, and if I told her too much she could scare the subject away. On the other hand, she seemed bright and levelheaded, and she deserved to get some more details for the kind of dough that she had paid me. Tough call.

A buzz clicked the gate open and I walked the gravel path to the main door. When Emma herself came to open the door, I was surprised.

"No servants?" I asked.

"It's their day off. It's actually better. Come in."

"And your husband?"

"Not at home."

"If you're all alone, you shouldn't open the gate like you did. It could be dangerous."

"We have a camera above the gate. I saw it was you."

We had walked from the door into a living room that was four times as big as my apartment. A nice fire was burning in the hearth, a short distance from a couple of leather armchairs. She motioned me to sit in one of them and took the second.

"So, are you bringing me some news?" she asked after a brief silence.

"Not really—well, I do have some, but it's nothing definitive."

"Tell me."

"I saw your husband go into a building in Chinatown. I don't know who he was meeting there and I couldn't find out because there was a disruption and he got away. So, in a sense, I don't have anything really new to relate, but I do have some questions."

"Ask away."

"First of all, I need to hear all you know about Al Zapowski."

"I've already told you all I know. I hired him to find out what my husband was doing. He said that this type of work was not in his league and referred me to you. That's it."

"Are you sure? Nothing else that he said or did? Can it be that he's being paid by your husband to mislead you? Could it be that all this ectoplasm thing is crap and he's having a good, old-fashioned affair with a living woman?"

"I'll answer you, but first, I haven't offered you anything to drink. How impolite of me! What will you have?"

"Bourbon on the rocks, thanks. I was getting kind of thirsty, now that you mention it."

Emma got up and approached a table loaded with bottles and glasses. I looked as she walked the distance to the table and couldn't help appreciating the grace of her gait. I had to remind myself that she was a client, not an acquaintance. When she returned and handed me the glass, instead of going back to her seat she stood before me. Somehow, that made me nervous, and I took a sip to hide it.

"The best way to answer your question is to show you, Dave," she said, and then she sat on my lap.

You could have knocked me down with a toothpick. This classy, demure woman had suddenly turned into a sexy bombshell. She took the glass from my hand and placed it on a side table without even looking at it, and then she placed her hand behind my neck. Her face was very close to mine and I felt her breath on my eyelids.

"What are you doing?" I asked. My voice was way more raucous than I would have liked it to be, but it was a miracle that I was able to speak at all.

"Showing you," she said, and then she got up and went placidly to sit in her armchair.

"Showing me?"

"Yes. Now I ask you, do you think that some other flesh-and-blood woman would be able to compete with me for my husband's attention?"

I considered it. I saw her point.

"Very unlikely, I admit it, but not impossible."

"No, not impossible, but for the time being I'm satisfied with 'very unlikely'. You've seen my husband's 'before' and 'after' pictures. I can think of no earthly woman who could make him lose weight that fast. I know, I've tried."

"All right. Let's proceed under the assumption that it is an ectoplasm. Do you have any idea when your husband goes to see her?"

"I think that he sees her every other day. He comes home

wasted and tells me that he's had a hard day at work, and the next day he stays in bed. On the third day it's the same story all over again. So, yes, every other day is my guess."

"This means that he should be coming home soon, if what I witnessed today was his regular meeting."

"He told me that he would come late. He has a business dinner or other. I wouldn't have risked having you in the house otherwise, but you need to leave pretty soon because you never know. I couldn't explain you to him. Any other questions?"

"Actually, I have a truckload of them. First of all, what do you plan to do when I confirm your suspicion?"

"I'll talk to him, and I'll try to help him kick the habit."

"And if you can't?"

She waited for a moment before answering, making what for a second looked to me like a theatrical pause.

"I have to succeed. If I can't, he'll be dead soon, if that ... thing keeps taking life away from him at that pace."

"You know, this is none of my business, but you are young and beautiful and you have all your life ahead of you. Why don't you divorce the creep and move on?"

"I couldn't live without him. Otto is the love of my life and I won't give up on him!"

She spoke vehemently and wiped her eye with her hand, as if to hide a tear. I can't cope with crying women and, anyway, it was no skin off my nose. I'd spoken sense to her for the last time, as far as I was concerned.

"I understand," I said. "I'll do my best to help. I should be going, now."

I got up and she saw me to the door without speaking. When I opened the door she placed a hand on my arm and gazed into my eyes.

"I need certainty, Dave. I can't confront him if I'm not certain, because he will deny everything and I won't have the strength to fight. Bring me certainty, please."

"I'll do my best," I said, and left. I'm not cut out for emotional scenes.

CHAPTER 5

I usually don't investigate my clients, once I have agreed to work for them. This time, however, I needed to know more about Emma. The sexy little show that she had given me had blown my mind away, because I had gotten a glimpse of a woman altogether different from the one I had agreed to take on as a client. I pride myself on being a good judge of character, but right then I didn't know what to make of Emma Wermeyer.

I had ruminated on it all quite a lot during a sleepless night. If Emma's guess was right, this was Wermeyer's day off from his sexual exploits, so I had time for some background work. I was alone; Daphne had waited for me at home that evening and after listening to a brief recap of my visit to Emma, sulking throughout it, she had said, "I'll be back," and gone she was. One less problem to worry about.

I knew where to go to start my inquiries. The offices of *The Gazette* were downtown, not far from my flat. Moreover, I had once gone out with Mariah, who manages the gossips page of the newspaper, and we still met on a friendly basis, every now and then. I decided to surprise her instead of calling ahead. Her door was open and she was absorbed in a paper. I knocked and she looked up, changing her puzzled expression into a smile. I like it when gals react to me like that.

"Well, well, well! See what the cat brought in," she said, getting up.

I approached and gave her a good kiss—one a bit north of brotherly, and she took it like a sport.

"Obviously you missed me and couldn't resist my attraction after only ... how long has it been, two months?" she said, jokingly.

"Yes, that of course, and also something else."

"What do you need, Dave? I've never seen you in the light of morning, if all you needed was my company."

"As a matter of fact, I need help. I'm trying to find some background information on one Emma Wermeyer. She must have featured in your gossips column, sometime or other."

"Is this interest professional, or personal?" she asked, lifting an eyebrow.

"Purely professional. Cross my heart and hope to die."

"All right. Then I'll help you. We actually worked on an extended piece on her. We invested a lot in research and with the material that our researcher brought to me I wrote a juicy piece, but then my editor axed it and it never got published."

"Why did he do that?"

"My guess? A fat check in one hand of your lady friend, and the promise of a lawsuit in the other. I never got a formal explanation, though, but I think that's pretty close to the truth."

"Okay. So what was in your piece?"

"Plenty. Let me find it for you," she said, and started to rummage through a bunch of folders she kept behind her desk. It took her less than two minutes to come up with a thin dossier.

"Here it is," she said, triumphantly.

I took it. It contained five closely typed pages and a few pictures and newspaper clippings.

"Can I read it?" I asked.

"Better, you can take it. Officially, it doesn't exist anymore. I was supposed to destroy it, but kind of 'forgot' to do it. But please, don't lose it and never tell anybody that you have it, if you don't want to get me fired."

"I promise. You're a sport, Mariah," I said, and gave her another of those not-so-brotherly kisses.

"When am I going to see you outside professional hours?" she asked with a sigh, when the kiss procedure was completed.

"As soon as this job I'm on is done. Promise. I owe you one."

"You owe me more than that," she said.

I nodded in assent. She's one of the best. I should see more of her.

I don't go to my office very often—there isn't much that I need there, and it isn't as if people dropped in to bring me work every day. This time, however, I needed the quiet I get at the office. The dead winged cockroach was still there and, to avoid future embarrassment, I kicked it out. It landed on the mat of my neighbor's office, the office of K. D. Watts, Certified Accountant. I smiled. I hate accountants.

I opened the file and spread the contents on my desk. The first item that got my attention was a big, black-and-white picture of a woman dancing on a pole. Her face was difficult to see, but I would have betted my suspenders that she was Emma. Other pictures showed Emma as a child, Emma in a bridal dress, together with a specimen I didn't recognize, and Emma with other assorted people. I started to read the piece written by Mariah and here's the gist of it. Emma's maiden name was O'Klarsky and she was born somewhere in the Midwest, but her family had moved to Vegas when she was eleven. Her father was an electrician, and her mother cleaned rooms at a local hotel. She got married to a Thomas Miller when she was twenty-three years old, and a year later she was a widow. The widowing process involved her husband carelessly walking off of a twentieth floor hotel balcony without a parachute. She was fast asleep at the time and had no idea how that had happened—or at least that was what a clipping from a local newspaper said.

Heart-broken Emma Miller had inherited a reasonable sum (but not huge, compared with the Wermeyer estate) from her deceased husband's life insurance, estimated at a couple million dollars. She had left Nevada because she couldn't cope with the sad memories. How sweet of her.

At the time of her marriage, Emma was working in a "show"—or in other words, she was doing strip tease. Mariah hinted, without saying so in so many words, that she was also known to be an escort and very popular with wealthy businessmen who frequented Vegas and its casinos. Little wonder that Emma had gone out of her way to suppress this article.

This information opened up a new train of thought. I had to know more and if that meant going to Vegas, so be it.

CHAPTER 6

The first class cabin was almost empty. I had bought a first class ticket with Emma's money, and felt no remorse for it. I hate flying and if I had to do it, at least I could do it in style. The flight attendant had removed my welcome drink, and I prepared to catch up on my sleep. I closed my eyes and got into the mood for a good nap, when a movement in the empty seat next to mine made me jump to attention. The seat was no longer empty and I was looking at the back of a passenger, who had covered herself with a blanket. I kept staring and the passenger turned toward me.

"This is really nice!" said Daphne.

"What the hell are you doing here?" I hissed between clenched teeth. "And how am I going to explain you to the flight attendant, if she comes along?"

"What's the fuss? I've never flown first class before. This is really classy, you know?"

"Listen to me," I said, trying to stay calm in spite of my exasperation, "I want you to get out of here, and I mean now!"

"Make me," she said, speaking softly.

"Oh, c'mon! You know as well as I do that we can't let anybody see you."

"Oh, that ... I won't, I promise."

Right then the flight attendant came walking along the aisle. With a little "whoosh," Daphne jumped into the magazine holder of my seat and made herself scarce just in time.

"Do you need anything, sir?" asked the attendant.

"No, nothing, thanks, I'm fine."

"I thought that you were saying something."

"No, no. Nothing, thanks. I just want to sleep. Please don't wake me up."

"Have a nice flight," she said, and left.

"See?" Daphne whispered from the magazine holder.

"Shut up, will you?" I whispered back. I turned around, drew my blanket over my head and went to sleep.

I like Vegas. It's different and makes you feel like you are free from your daily worries. It's the lights, I think. I don't go out a lot during the day because it is scorching hot, so most of my Vegas memories are at night. I had taken a room at the Venetian, which is as phony as the rest of them, but at least there you can get good chocolate and I'm a chocolate addict. I also like to walk through the casino, but I'll never give them a penny. You can't beat the machine. I resisted the temptation to use Daphne's help to bust the blackjack table. I try to be honest when I can. Daphne just shrugged when I refused, but her face expressed her disdain at my lack of enterprise.

Before leaving home I had contacted Mark Seaver, the reporter who had written the piece on Miller's accidental death, and he had agreed to meet with me the next morning, so I had to kill time that night. I sat in my room, thumbing through the various brochures and offers, when Daphne manifested herself. I hadn't seen her since refusing her offer to cheat on the casino, and I was hoping that she wouldn't be around for a while, but there she was.

"What are you planning to do?" she asked.

"If you need to know it—and I'm not sure why you think that you need to know it—I plan to have a quiet dinner and then go to a show."

"Which one?"

I paused for a minute to think. Why was this dead person interested in the show that I was planning to go to, and why was I even discussing it with her? But I couldn't read anything sinister in her question, so I answered it.

"I was thinking to go to this concert here," I said, showing the ad to her. "It's a new singer that I really like."

"I have heard that there is a really good water acrobatics show. Why don't you go to see that?"

"Because that's not what I planned."

"Would you consider changing your plan? Please? Really, really please?"

"What's going on, Daphne?"

She kept silent for a moment and then she raised her head. She had a pleading expression on her face that I hadn't seen before.

"I always wanted to see that show, but never had an opportunity to go. I would be really grateful to you if you agreed to take me."

"I don't get you," I said, and I didn't. "You can go wherever you like. You don't need me. So I'll go to my concert and you can go to this show. What's the problem?"

I've seen ghosts look embarrassed before, but Daphne wasn't

the type. She was always cheeky and outspoken. Still, without doubt she was doing the ectoplasmic equivalent of shuffling her feet.

"I ... feel ... uncomfortable, going places alone. I need company. I need people around me, people that I can trust and talk to. If I go alone to a public place, I feel lost. I can't explain it, but there it is."

You live and learn. She sounded truly worried and her concern was obviously genuine. A shy dead whore? Or just a lost soul, who knows ...

"All right. I'll take you to the water acrobatics show, but it better be good," I said, trying to sound severe.

"Thank you, thank you, thank you!" Daphne yelled, and before I could stop her, she jumped at me and pasted a big kiss on my forehead. That wasn't too bad, I must admit. It didn't make me shiver as the contact with ghosts usually does, so I didn't complain.

The show was quite decent and I had a good time. Daphne had kept hidden in my jacket pocket, from which she had a good view of the show. After the show I went straight back to the hotel and to bed. It had been a long day.

In the morning, I called Mark and we agreed to meet for breakfast at Grand Lux Café at The Venetian. I've never seen anybody eat that much at breakfast. He had a three-egg omelet and a pile of toast with butter and honey, all washed down with a big pot of coffee, and then he really dug into it and ordered pancakes and some other garbage I couldn't identify. I watched with awe as he wolfed everything down like someone who hadn't eaten in a week. When he was through and working on his second pot of coffee, I felt entitled to ask him as many questions as I needed to.

"So," he said. Not a question, just the word.

"I appreciate your taking the time to meet with me," I said. Always a good policy to sound thankful.

"My pleasure," he said. He looked around the table as if to make sure that there was no crumb that he had forgotten to ingest, and seeing that the plates were empty he reclined back to start digesting the muck.

"I understand that you were on the spot when Thomas Miller took his last dive?" I prompted him.

"You bet. I was covering another story, when out of nowhere this man hits the pavement."

"What can you tell me that wasn't in your printed report?"

"A lot. Everything that wasn't fit for printing unless we were courting a lawsuit for defamation."

"I'm listening."

"The woman, Emma, she's a piece of work."

"I know that. I've met her."

"What you don't know is that she's slept around, and with some useful people, too. One of them is a certain judge, who prohibited the performance of an autopsy on the ground that it violated the religious belief of the deceased. The evidence of this alleged religious belief was the widow's testimony. None of his friends ever heard of it and it couldn't be confirmed in any other way. Nevertheless, the body was cremated in a hurry. The police did not find any indication that the death was other than an accident or suicide and the case was closed. The widow got the insurance money really quick, and then she left."

"Why couldn't it be an accident or a suicide?" I pressed.

"I'm not saying it wasn't, but I don't believe it for a second. To jump from that balcony one had to climb a high rail, and that's not something you do by mistake, unless you're hallucinating under the influence of some drug. As for the suicide, only a day before his death he had bought a new sports car, a cool convertible. Tell me what man would jump to his death before he's had a chance of driving something like that."

"You have a point. We can rule out suicide, and an accident is difficult to swallow."

"And, of course, there is the matter of the insurance."

"Which matter of the insurance?"

"The policy was taken just a month before the event—by his wife. She was the only beneficiary. His parents got squat."

"That sounds fishy, I agree."

"I rest my case. Well, I have to go," he said. I thanked him for his time and went back to my room a very pensive person.

As soon as I closed the door behind me, Daphne materialized. "She pushed him," she said.

"We shouldn't jump to conclusions," I pointed out. "We only heard the story from the point of view of a reporter. The facts may be quite different."

"The facts are that she's a bitch, as I told you," Daphne insisted. "So now what?"

"Now we go back and start all over again."

CHAPTER 7

The return flight was uneventful and I got home just in time for a bite to eat, a shower, and a good sleep. Daphne had been silent most of the time, which suited me fine. At the apartment, she once again took position by the window and gave me her back. I wondered what she was looking at, but decided not to inquire.

I got up late the next morning and as soon as I felt human again—meaning, after a good cup of coffee and a shower—I dialed Emma's number. She was quick to answer.

"Yes?" her musical voice said.

"It's me"

"Where have you been? I called you twice." She sounded annoyed.

"Working on the case. Listen, today I plan to follow your husband as he leaves home, on the off chance that he may have changed the location of his meeting. At what time does he leave home?"

"You're late. He has already left."

"Damn! Well, let's hope that he's sticking to the same meeting place. I'll be in touch."

"Dave ..."

"Yes?"

"Bring me certainty. Bring it to me today. I can't go on like this for much longer."

"I'll do my best," I said, and hung up.

The number one problem I had was that I didn't know at what time Wermeyer would be meeting his hooker. If they kept a regular schedule it would be in the late afternoon, but I would have to keep watch all day behind that dumpster to make sure I didn't miss him, and that was out of the question. Then the solution presented itself to me.

"Daphne," I called. "Do you ever get bored?"

"Bored? No, why?"

"Because we are partners, right? So here is where you really start to help me. I need you to keep guard by that dumpster and to come get me when Wermeyer arrives. I'll be in a nearby place. Okay?"

"So now poor little Daphne is useful, right? When you can exploit me all of a sudden I'm your partner, but after I do my part you'll tell me again how useless I am, won't you?"

"No way! Why would you say that? We surely are partners and partners help each other out. So will you do this little chore for me?"

"Yeah, yeah. I'll do it. It's not that I have much else to do anyway. Let's go."

I found a dark bar with a private enough booth to wait in, only a minute away from that dumpster. I sped Daphne on her way and ordered beer and French fries to while away the time. The hours passed and I got sleepy, but when Daphne woke me up by shouting into my ear, it was entirely uncalled for.

"He's arrived. Wake up!" she yelled.

I jumped to my feet, left five dollars on the table to take care of the tab, and strode out as fast as I could without actually running. A minute later we were once again behind that dumpster. The same unmistakable sounds came from the second floor window.

"What happened? Tell me," I commanded.

"Nothing special. He arrived and went up and I came to get you. And, by the way, there is no ectoplasm there now either."

This thing was starting to get on my nerves and I decided to end it right then and there.

"Come with me," I said.

I pulled my revolver from its holster and ran up the stairs without planning ahead too much, until I reached a door that did little to muffle the loud moans coming from within. I never had a prejudice against breaking and entering, so I kicked the door in and made an entrance, gun first. Daphne's statement checked out. There was no ectoplasm in the room. The loud moans came from a tape recorder and Otto Wermeyer, who was seated at a small table drinking bourbon from a large glass, took no part in them. Only he wasn't Otto Wermeyer at all, if you get my drift. Now that I saw him in good light I was sure of it. He bore a good resemblance to Wermeyer, but wasn't him. He was the man in the second photograph that Emma gave me, but was no Otto.

"What ..." he started to say but when his gaze fell on my gun he froze.

"Who are you? What's your name?" I threw at him.

"Bill Barnes. What are you, the police?"

"I'm asking the questions. Where is Otto Wermeyer?"

"I know nothing of this Otto of yours. I'm only paid to come here every other day and do this routine. I sit here for an hour until the tape ends and then I go. The pay is good and I ask no questions. I haven't done anything illegal and you have nothing against me."

"Who's paying you?"

He shrugged. "I don't know his surname. Al something. A fat one. I met him in a place downtown where you don't ask too many questions."

"Zapowski!" I yelled.

"No need to be abusive, you know?" said Barnes, looking hurt.

"Listen," I said, taking advantage of his assumption that I was the police. "If you don't want to get in trouble with us this is what you do. You go straight back home and speak with nobody. Clear? First let me see some ID."

The poor guy nodded, swallowed quickly and handed me a driver's license with his name on it. I wrote the details in my notebook—the one I keep to impress gullible people—and nodded.

"Beat it!" I ordered.

Barnes made a beeline for the door. He obviously was happy to get off lightly.

"Don't leave town," I shouted after him. I had always wanted to say that to somebody.

A blurry image materialized into Daphne and she faced me, smiling smugly.

"Told you so," she said. "Hey, is that bourbon? It's been ages since I tasted some. I wish I could ..."

"We have no time to waste," I said, moving quickly to the door. "We must go to Wermeyer's house."

"What for? You've lost me here," said Daphne, twitching the tip of her nose.

"That's why I'm the detective and you're ... whatever," I pointed out.

CHAPTER 8

The Wermeyers did themselves well and their house, located in the classiest neighborhood in town, stood in the middle of rolling grounds surrounded by a security wall. When we reached the gate, Daphne did her disappearing act again and I started to work on the gate lock, but first I hung my hat on the camera to blind it, although its purpose was to identify callers, and I wasn't going to ring no bells. The lock was a new model so I had to sweat a bit to make it click, and I had just got inside and closed the gate behind me when Daphne reappeared.

"Are you going to take all night, Dave?" she complained.

"I'm still solid flesh, you know," I answered, a little peeved by her attitude. "What did you find?"

"The cellar, I think," she answered somewhat cryptically, and without another word she started to float toward the house. I had little choice but to follow.

A servant was in the backyard, smoking her head off; she had left the kitchen door unlocked and it was the work of a moment for us to run through the kitchen and down a flight of stairs to the cellar.

The cellar had a thick wooden door that was locked and blocked us, but not for long; I always carry with me the set of keys that a sentimental, now ex-girlfriend, gave me for my birthday. In less than a minute the lock was picked and we walked into a cold and damp wine cellar that was larger than my apartment and office combined. As we got used to the dim light we noticed a bundle of clothes on the floor, next to a variety of empty wine bottles. It startled me when the bundle stirred and on closer inspection turned out to be Otto Wermeyer. Among the empty bottles that were strewn around him I noticed several pricey French wines, along with brands I didn't know.

"Mister Wermeyer," I called, and he opened two watery eyes that he fixed on me.

"Bru ... blu ... ah," he said.

"Can you hear me, Mister Wermeyer? Are you okay?"

"Tell my wife that I'm in the shellar ... in she-sellar ... locked in shellar," he mumbled.

Apparently Wermeyer had been feeding on alcohol for quite some time and was in no state to talk coherently to us. Not that he didn't try, but all he was able to produce after those few enlightening words were slurred sounds and Claret-scented bubbles. Suddenly more lights were switched on and I heard steps. We had company.

"Dave ... what are you doing here? How did you get in?" said Emma, who was plainly not too pleased to see me.

"Grab the bitch," Daphne's voice whispered in my ear.

"What did you say?" Emma asked, clearly puzzled.

"I didn't say anything ..."

"But *I* did, you bitch," said Daphne, materializing in a flash.

Her appearance made quite an impression on Emma who turned a beautiful red.

"... with your saint-like act," Daphne continued.

"Enough, Daphne," I said.

"... while all the while you were plotting and scheming, as they say ..."

"Shut up, Daphne!" I ordered, and this time she did.

"Dave," said Emma, wearing an angelic expression and getting really close to me, "I have no idea what this is all about, believe me."

She grabbed my arm and squeezed it hard, gazing at me with her innocent, blue eyes.

"The game is over, Emma," I said, as gently as I could. "We know that you came to me simply to cook up an alibi so I could testify that you were a devoted wife, while all the time you kept your husband in the cellar, destined to starve to death. And I know that Zapowski is working with you and is in this up to his neck. There is no point in denying it."

I must hand it to Emma—she was a tough cookie. She pulled herself together quickly and started offering me money, which I would have liked to take, but couldn't. *Noblesse oblige*, like them Canadians like to say.

"Name your price to forget all this and I'll pay it. Here," she said, pulling out her checkbook and starting to write a sum with more zeros in it than I could count, "take this and go away. Take that freaky thing with you and forget that you ever saw me."

I took the check and gazed at it with sadness. "I'd love to," I said, quite sincerely, "but I'll have to pass, this time."

At this point Emma apparently realized that arguing was going to get her nowhere. She shook her head and before I could stop her she dashed up the stairs and in a moment was gone. It didn't take a genius to understand that the roar of the engine that we heard a minute later meant that she had left the premises in a hurry. Daphne looked at me accusingly and I shrugged.

"Not our problem. Let her go," I said. We had more pressing items on our agenda, namely Otto Wermeyer.

"You're okay, now, Mister Wermeyer. You'll be fine," I reassured him.

Wermeyer had sobered up a little and now seemed to appreciate the situation.

"My wife ... she locked me in here, right? And she wanted to kill me. And you saved me, right?"

"That's it, in a nutshell," I agreed.

"And that check, let me see it."

I gave him the check that Emma had scribbled and to my surprise, instead of tearing it up he took a golden pen from his inner pocked and signed it.

"I've endorsed it," he said. "Now you can cash it."

Having said that, he went back to sleep with loud snores. I picked him up, carried him to his bedroom and took care of him. I needed him to stay well, at least for a little while longer, to make sure that my check wouldn't bounce.

The job ended well. Emma and Zapowski were picked up by the police after Otto Wermeyer got sober again and told them how she had planned to murder him and make his death look like the result of his alleged extramarital affair. Otto was *really* grateful and tripled the check that Emma had given me, so I don't have to work for a while and can take it easy.

And Daphne ... well, I began to like her, after a while, particularly when she made good on her word, so she comes to visit every so often. I must watch against liking it too much though; I think I'm starting to lose weight.

EPISODE THREE

MICE

CHAPTER 1

"Where the hell are they coming from?"

When Frankie asked a question, it always sounded like he was placing the blame on someone—me, in this case. Instead of answering, I squashed the white mouse that had just climbed out of his coffee cup. The mouse had the consistency of putty and felt like it; no bloodshed was involved in the squashing.

I needed time to think. Fiddling with the mouse wouldn't buy me much time, though, because as soon as a white mouse was reduced to a flat pulp, another one popped up somewhere else. This time, one materialized on Frankie's shoulder and stood there, gazing at me reproachfully.

"That wasn't a very nice thing to do, Mr. Callaghan," it said with its feminine, squeaky voice. "That blow hurt my brother; you know that, right?"

I ignored it and turned my attention back to Frankie, who was giving signs of impatience. Pacifying him was my top priority.

"What do they want?" he asked, speaking more petulantly than before.

"They wouldn't say," I answered, as if he didn't know that.

"I hired you to find out, remember?"

Well, yes …… if sending a couple of ugly goons to yank me out of bed in the middle of the night counted as hiring, then he had hired me.

I gazed at Frankie Leone and didn't like what I saw. I could tell that he was badly pissed off and his red face, with its orange-peel look and porcine eyes, was uglier than ever. His fat body quivered and he jerked his left knee incessantly. He was hideous, even considering that he was a dangerous mafioso. Left alone, I would never have dreamt of working for him, but I wasn't given a vote.

"Be patient, Frankie," I pleaded. "I'm working on it and will find something soon."

"No, he won't," squealed the white mouse; I grabbed it harder than I had to and put it in the small cage that I had brought with me.

"He says you won't," said Frankie, speaking dangerously.

"It's a mouse, for gosh sake!" I pointed out. "You can't go by what it says."

"Look here, Callaghan. You must make them go away. They are ruining my business. They pop up while I talk about delicate operations. Yesterday I was discussing a shipment of quality material with one of my West Coast cousins and this mouse pops up and keeps telling him that the police are after him and that the shipment will cost him twenty years in the clink. After that he was running so fast that you couldn't see his dust."

"I know, I know," I said, trying to sound really sympathetic.

"And I can't get any sleep either. Last night I woke up to find one of those things reciting 'Mary had a little lamb' to me. You must stop it, and now ain't soon enough."

"Certainly," I said, dutifully. "I'm doing my best."

"Well, you do your best and rid me of them before the end of this week, or I'll have to get a new private eye."

"A new PE?" I echoed, swallowing with difficulty. When Frankie took on a new employee, you had to dig in the concrete blocks at the bottom of the bay to find the old ones.

"Yup!"

I started to put together a plea for more time—considerably

more time—but that was when Lena, Frankie's wife, walked in, taking my breath away. I had never seen her before but I had heard that she was astonishingly beautiful, although nothing could ever prepare me for the real thing. The thought that she was married to a piece of cheese like Frankie was difficult to digest.

"Are you done, Honey? You promised to take me to that new boutique."

"No, I'm not. Go away! Can't you see that I'm busy talking business?"

"Oh, but I get sooo bored, Love! And you know that it's bad for my skin."

"Then tell Boris to take you. What do I pay bodyguards for?"

"OK, I'll go with Boris. But you aren't cross, Sweetie, are you?"

"No, no. Go!" he said, and turned to me.

I was amazed. This broad had just called the toughest gangster this side of the river "Sweetie" in the presence of a witness and got away with it without a murmur. I hadn't thought it could be done. Perhaps the mice were sapping Frankie of his toughness. But that, apparently, didn't apply to his approach to me.

"Now get the hell outa here and get busy!" he ordered.

I got up, taking the small cage with me.

"I'll do my best," I repeated stupidly once again, as I stood at the door. "And ... ehr ... you have a mouse in your hair," I concluded, closing the door behind me quickly enough for the new mouse that Frankie had just thrown, to crush against it with a thud.

I sat in my car with the cage on the passenger's seat and gazed at the mouse, which was sniffing the air seraphically.

"What are you? Who's sending you?"

"Ah, you would like to know that, wouldn't you?"

"'Like' is not the word. I *need* to find out. Do you know what will happen to me if I don't?"

"Did you know that the average distance from the Earth to the Moon is 384,403 kilometers or 238,857 miles?"

"Do you know how long it will take you to die if I throw this cage into the river?"

"You go ahead and do that, and then try to solve this mystery all by yourself."

I felt a sudden glimpse of hope. "So you will help me?"

"I didn't say that."

"Then you're not going to help me."

"I didn't say that either."

I took the cage and threw it to the back of the car. I hoped it had hurt.

CHAPTER 2

I had heard of the Cornflakes Oracle before, but I had never been so desperate as to go and see her. This time, however, I was in the worst fix ever and was willing to try anything. The man who opened the door was an ugly specimen, fat, pimpled, and slightly hunchbacked. He took a long look at me and then waved me in.

"I'm here to see the Oracle," I said.

He smiled a horrible, toothless smile and nodded.

"You're lucky," he said. "She's having puffed rice today."

"How so?"

"The messages are much clearer with the puffed rice than with the corn flakes, I can tell you that. It's two hundred dollars."

"Can't you give me a discount? I only have a simple question."

He grimaced at my question and put a hand out. I paid.

"Wait here," he said, and soon he came back carrying a white plate and motioned to me to follow him into an adjacent room. The Cornflakes Oracle was seated on a throne-like armchair and was intent on eating Coco-Pops from a large bowl. She was fatter and uglier than her usher, with long, black hair that dipped in the milk every time she moved her head. The sounds that she made eating do not bear repeating.

"Say nothing," said the man. "She knows your question already. Watch here for the answer," he added and placed the white plate close to the bowl.

The Cornflakes Oracle took a large spoonful of puffed cocoa rice, wet with milk, and spread it on the white plate.

"Here's your answer," said the assistant, thrusting the plate at me.

I gaped at him, not knowing what to make of it, until I saw that the chocolate-colored rice had formed letters and words on the plate. The words said, "Play Beethoven, Hide Mouse, Go Venetian." I couldn't make heads or tails of it.

"What does it mean?"

"Ha!" said the assistant, and then he pushed me out of the room. He was flaccid but heavy and I found myself outside.

"You got what you paid for. Go and make good use of it," he said, and then he pushed me again, out of the house, and closed the door in my face.

On the way home I started to think that there might be something in the Oracle's advice. For one thing, she knew that I had a problem with mice and her advice could still turn out to be to the point. I knew I had a CD of Beethoven somewhere in the house; it took me only a few minutes to find it. I took the mouse's cage and brought it to the living room where I kept my audio system.

"You went around wasting some time?" it asked me, as soon as I put the cage down.

"That we'll see," I said, and I hit "play." The sounds of Beethoven's Emperor piano concert filled the air. A shriek came from the cage and I saw that the mouse was doing contortions in it. I hit the "stop" button and the contortions stopped.

"Brute! Cruel!" yelled the mouse.

"What, don't you like Beethoven? Perhaps you haven't listened to it long enough to acquire a taste for it," I said, and hit the "play" button again.

The mouse got into contortions again and I hit "stop" again.

"Please, please, stop that torture. It's done!"

"What is done?"

"I don't know how you found out, but playing Beethoven at me released the block that prevented me from helping you. But don't make me listen to it anymore; from now on it will only be pointless torture."

"So now you will tell me what I need?"

"I'll do what I can," said the mouse in a low voice.

"All right, start talking."

"Listen, this is the deal: I can't give you any direct answer because if I do I'll be destroyed immediately. I can help with hints, but nothing more than that. It doesn't matter how much Beethoven you play to me, that's all I can do."

"Uhmm ... I'm not sure that I believe you. Why would you want to help me?"

"I can't explain that either, remember? No direct answers."

"A fat lot of good that's gonna do me. So what's your next hint?"

"If someone wanted to destroy me, wouldn't you think that it would be in your best interest to keep me safe?"

"Hide the mouse" was what the Oracle had said, so perhaps it made sense. The mouse was hinting that someone wanted to kill it, which apparently was not a good thing for me—although I had wanted to kill it myself—and so I was to hide it to keep it safe. I was starting to feel more respect for the Oracle, after the Beethoven thing had produced results. But what about the rest of the message?

"Someone said 'go Venetian' to me. Can you make anything of that?"

"The Venetian is a well-known hotel in Las Vegas, which reproduces the atmosphere of the Italian city of Venice. 'Venetian' may also refer to a type of blinds, widely used in construction ..."

"Stop!" I threw at the mouse. I was exasperated by its habit of bringing up irrelevant details. The mouse ignored me and continued to speak.

"... 'Venetian' may also refer to a themed nightclub, located downtown, where private and public events are organized in the spirit of the Venice Carnival."

The mouse stopped and gazed at me conspiratorially, and then I understood.

"I have to go somewhere," I said, grabbing the cage, "but first I'll drop you off at a safe place."

CHAPTER 3

The Venetian was located in a narrow street and had an unpretentious entrance with few lights and a poster showing a couple dressed up for Carnival. Finding a safe place for the mouse had taken me time, but after much convincing I had managed to talk Lizzy into stuffing it in one of her closets. Elizabeth—Lizzy to her friends—was a former girlfriend with whom I still was on chummy terms. More than that, actually; we still had a thing for each other and spent time together in the sack quite often, but she sternly refused to link her future with mine as long as I didn't get myself a steady job, which in her vocabulary meant slaving 10 hours a day at some boring desk job. Not my thing. Lizzy was a great gal, but she had a degree in arts and was a guide at the museum of modern arts—not my thing either.

The hour was still early, close to 10 PM, and I wondered why the area was quiet, almost deserted. Without hesitating I pushed the glass door and walked into the badly lit foyer. A young woman dressed in a Venetian seventeenth-century-style dress took my hat and coat in exchange for a numbered chip and showed me the way into the nightclub.

I approached the bar and climbed the stool. I needed to give myself time to get used to the lighting. The room was full of young people and everybody wore Venetian ball masks, which made me stand out. The barman came to take my order and pushed a mask at me. "Everybody has to wear one," he said, "and this simple one is on the house."

I checked it and saw that it was a cheap plastic piece, but it would do. I put it on and aimed a plastic smile at the barman. "Thanks. A gin and tonic to go with this would be perfect," I said. I'm usually a scotch person, but I needed to stay sharp.

Armed with the mask and my drink, I decided to explore the place. Small groups of people were scattered around, chatting, and couples were dancing at the sound of a pretty decent live band. In one corner other people were sitting on black leather seats and from one of those black holes a heavenly creature stood up, attracting my full attention. She wore black tights from her feet to her neck, leaving nothing to imagination as far as curves were concerned. She had a perfect body and she knew how to animate it. You had to be brain-dead to be able to keep your eyes off her. She had long, blonde hair and her face was hidden by a Venetian mask—the real thing, not a cheap plastic surrogate—with silver and diamonds on a black background and a white feather on one side. She looked vaguely familiar, like a supermodel or a movie star, and I kept staring at her as she walked straight to me.

"Hi. You seem to be all alone," she said, blinding me with a smile.

I took a quick sip of my drink, taking time to think of a clever repartee. "Yeah, and I forgot my sunglasses, so please ring your bell before you smile again," I finally said, feeling smart.

That got me another smile from her, and as she flashed her white teeth at me I said, more somberly, "This is my first time here. I'm just getting used to the place."

"You can buy me a drink while you do that. Perhaps I can help you to find your way around. I'm an old timer."

I considered the offer. I hadn't come here to let some hostess trick me into spending more money. I knew how the trick worked: you bought her an expensive drink and she got water in her glass. The place made a good profit on the sucker, who was happy to be drinking in the company of a beautiful girl. Only I didn't like being the sucker. Still, I was here to gather information and this woman might have some, which could be worth the price.

"Why not? Let's go to the bar," I said.

"Better, let's sit over here. I'll go and get us drinks. What would you like?"

She piloted me toward one of the black couches and I sat down, sinking into it.

"I'll have scotch on the rocks," I said.

She nodded and turned away. I watched her walk to the bar, enjoying the fluidity of her body's movements, and then I watched her walk back. I kept trying to remember why she looked familiar to me, but watching her was too distracting for me to concentrate. She came back bringing two glasses, hers with a pinkish liquid in it, and when she gave me my scotch her fingers touched my hand, quickly sending electricity running along my arm. She sat down beside me and raised her glass for a toast.

"Your health," she said.

"Yours," I echoed.

I gulped down a good half of my drink, but the liquor had barely reached my stomach when my vision became blurred and my ears started to buzz. I dropped my glass, and I looked at her in disbelief.

"You slipped me a Mickey Finn!"

"Yeah, a shame, ah?"

"Like a bloody tenderfoot ... "

"Yep," she said, nodding in assent, and that's the last thing I saw before passing out.

CHAPTER 4

I woke up slowly, in stages. The first thing I saw was a ceiling, so clearly I was lying face up. Testing my extremities, I realized that my hands and legs were tied to what seemed to be a bed. The gorgeous woman from the bar was sitting on me, still wearing her Venetian mask. I wouldn't have objected to the kinky set up, normally, except that she was fully clothed and was slapping me in the face.

"Wake up!" she ordered between slaps.

"Hey, stop it!" I managed to say.

She stopped the slapping routine and climbed off me.

"You took your sweet time waking up," she complained.

My head was clearing and I was starting to get my priorities right again.

"Untie me," I said.

"Yeah, sure," she said, mockingly. "As soon as you give me what I need, I'll untie you."

"I don't have anything of value. Just a few bucks and you can take those."

She sat on the bed beside me, her face close to mine, and gazed into my eyes as if to gauge if I was lying.

"I'm no thief and you know that. You have something that belongs to my organization and I need it. Where is it?"

"Lady, I've no idea what you're talking about. You must be thinking of some other guy."

"No, Mr. Callaghan ... or can I call you Dave?" Without waiting for a response she continued. "You see, Dave, I really need that mouse that you're keeping. It's not your property and you have no use for it, while for me it is extremely important. So here's the deal: you tell me where the mouse is and as soon as I find it, I'll tell my men to come and cut you loose. Deal?"

So that was it. I had stirred up something by taking that mouse, but I was damned if I was going to hand it over to this woman.

"First of all, what's your name?"

"You can call me Fairy."

"Sure, you look like one," I said, smiling my most accommodating smile. "Now take off that mask. I like to see who I'm dealing with."

"That won't happen. And if you failed to notice, you're in no position to dictate. In your place, I would be scared to death."

"That's because, unlike me, you wouldn't have realized immediately that you're a Fed."

That was a long shot, but I could have sworn that she wasn't one of the bad guys. Call it intuition, but also a good reading of the map. There were no goons in the room, ready to get information from me with red-hot pincers, which in those circles is the preferred way to make recalcitrant people talk.

She was clearly taken aback, and I thought that she even blushed a bit.

"How did you know?"

"That's why I am a detective. Now untie me."

"Not yet. It's true that I am with the law, but I'm not so sure that I can trust you."

"You can trust me. Scout's word."

"The last guy who told me that, I had to shoot between the eyes. I won't take chances with you, but I'll trust you a little.

"I belong to a special branch that you have never heard of and the very existence of which you must forget. It was originally set up as an army unit that was to counter a similar organization that existed in the Soviet Union. Later it was turned into a civil organization and included people with many talents. We had far-seers, telepaths, and some people with weird abilities that we weren't even sure how useful they might be. One of those recruits was Anne. She had one peculiar ability: she was able to create small ectoplasms anywhere on the globe, from afar, and to project herself into them. As you can imagine, this presented endless possibilities as far as intelligence was concerned.

"At first Anne only managed to make shapeless objects, but with time and training she learned to create ectoplasms in the shape of mice. Then, one day two years ago, she disappeared. We are sure that she was kidnapped and have been looking for her everywhere. The mice that started plaguing your employer are the first sign of life that we have gotten from her, so you understand why it is so important for me to get hold of that mouse."

"How did you know that I would be coming to the Venetian?"

"We've been following you and learned what the Cornflakes Oracle told you. The rest was easy."

"You seem to know an awful lot about me and my doings, and you also sound unprofessionally involved in this story, which makes me wonder."

"You're right. Anne is my cousin and she was under my protection when she was kidnapped. So you can understand why I'm so worked up about it."

"I understand and sympathize, but I can't help you. The mouse was useless to me and I let it go. I'm sorry. But I'm sure that you can get another one where that one came from."

Sure, I was lying. I hadn't bought the story—at least not in its entirety, and I wasn't going to let that mouse out of my control.

"Damn! I was so close ..."

"Yeah, I'm sorry. But will you untie me now? These cords are cutting into my wrists."

"Not right now," she said. She got up from the bed and walked to the door. "I've got things to do," she added before walking out. "Someone will take care of you."

"Hey!" I yelled, but she had already left.

I waited; what else could I do? After a while the door opened and a young man walked in. He wore a black outfit with silver and fake diamonds, and sported a Venetian mask.

"Wow! You've been wild, ah? How come your lady forgot to untie you?" He blabbered as he untied me and I let him. When at last I was free again I was in no charitable mood.

"Can't you see that I'm fully dressed? What does that tell you?"

"Oh, but this lady called and said that she had forgotten to untie you and you were asleep in this courtesy room and would I please come to untie you, and so I thought ..."

"Moron!" I spat and stormed out of the room. I had no patience left.

CHAPTER 5

I was hungry, but getting the mouse back came first on my to-do list. Lizzy was out and I let myself in with the key that she had let me keep. The cage and the mouse were still where I had left them and I brought them to the kitchen where I fixed myself a big sandwich and a beer, and then I sat at the kitchen table to eat and gazed at the mouse.

"Do you eat?" I asked.

"I don't need to," said the mouse, speaking disdainfully.

"Why are you so special? Why you of all the white mice that are plaguing Frankie?"

"Ah, you would like to know that, wouldn't you?"

"Don't start again!" I admonished it.

The mouse was gazing at me so superciliously that I had to do something about it.

"I think I'll start to call you Anne. That's your name, right?"

White mice don't go white in the face, but I could have sworn that it had paled.

"How ... how did you find out?"

"I have ways."

"But how?"

"Ah, you would like to know that, wouldn't you?" I had waited for an opportunity to say that back to the mouse.

"Oh, it doesn't matter," said the mouse, "I'm not sure that anything matters anymore." She sounded sad.

"Listen," I said, and meant to interrogate it for as long as it took to get the information I needed out of it, but right then all hell broke loose. The kitchen window's glass shattered into pieces and machine gun bullets started decorating Lizzy's kitchen. I dropped to the floor, taking the cage with me. Lizzy's apartment is on the first floor and the bullets were coming at an angle from the street so I was relatively safe as long as I kept low. I started to creep toward the living room and away from the street window, but when a hand grenade came through it I got up and ran. The grenade exploded just as I passed through the door.

"They want to kill us," the mouse shrieked.

"You don't say," I said, bitterly.

"Let me out of the cage, please!"

I leaned against the wall trying to catch my breath.

"Sure, so you can run away from me."

"No, I promise. You have my word that I won't run away, but I need to be free in case you get killed."

That made some sense—not the getting killed part, the other part—and at this point I needed to take some chances if I wanted to get anywhere with this investigation.

"No time to argue now. Here, get into my inner pocket and hold tight," I ordered, fishing the mouse from the cage.

I opened the door of Lizzy's apartment, checked that there was nobody in sight and took the stairs to the higher floors. I knew from previous experience that there was a way to get to the building next to Lizzy's from the roof, because on two occasions I had used her apartment to shake tails. The door to the roof was unlocked, and I got away easily. I didn't go back to see who was after me; curiosity never pays.

CHAPTER 6

Milt had finished locking the doors and barring the windows, and if he was surprised to see me talking to a white mouse, he didn't show it. Milt was my friend and mentor, and I owed him everything I knew about detecting. I had started my career working for him, and when he had finally decided to retire from active work, I had kept the agency running. We saw each other often, most of the time in his little pub by the pier in which we were sitting now. The pub was almost always empty of customers, but I knew that Milt didn't mind because he kept it as a façade for his real business, which involved trafficking in goods the nature of which I would rather not discuss.

I sat at one of the small wooden tables, bringing with me the bottle of scotch that I had taken from the bar. I still felt shaky and needed it. The mouse had jumped out of my inner pocket and was now on the table, facing me.

"I see you have a jukebox," she said, addressing Milt.

"I sure do," answered Milt, as if speaking with white mice were an everyday business for him.

"Elvis," the mouse said quickly.

"What?" Said Milt.

." . .'lvis," the mouse hissed.

"Play some Elvis on the jukebox," I told Milt. I thought I understood what the mouse was driving at and became sure when it nodded emphatically.

As soon as the first notes of "In the Ghetto" filled the air, the mouse came closer and started talking.

"Listen," she said, "as long as Elvis is playing I can speak freely. Tell your friend to keep it going."

I got up and explained it to Milt. He nodded and took position by the jukebox. That was Milt all right, not wasting time with silly questions. I got back to the table and sat down. "Start talking," I said.

"I don't know how much you know, so stop me if I'm telling you stuff you've heard before," the mouse started, speaking in a conspiratorially low undertone. "As you know, my name is Anne. I am psychic, and I had been working with the government for two years before I got kidnapped. What you see now—the mouse—is a projection of my mind."

"I knew that much, and I met your cousin ..."

"Oh, so that's where you know my name from. Anyway, I don't know how they learned about me, but one day three hooded men with guns broke into my so-called 'safe apartment' and kidnapped me. I've been held in a basement since then."

"Who are these people? Can you describe them to me?"

"No, I'm sorry. They were always hooded when they came into the basement and used a device to alter their voices. I couldn't even tell you if they are foreigners or aliens from Mars."

"Where is the basement? How do I get there?"

"I don't actually know, although I know who knows—but leave that for later; I need to tell you everything first."

"All right, hurry up."

"So they kept me in the basement; they knew exactly what I was able to do and they forced me to help them. It was all done very quietly, and I was ordered to send a mouse here and a mouse there, to collect information and bring it back to them. One of the assignments I got was really bad, and I decided not to help them; instead, I brought back wrong information, but they found out and I got punished."

"How did they find out?"

"They have a machine—I don't know how it works—with electrodes that they connect to my body and they use it to eavesdrop on my remote conversations done via the mouse."

"But that means that are listening to us right now and we're in danger," I said, starting to get up and looking around instinctively.

"No, no. As I told you, as long as we keep Elvis playing, they can't hear what we're saying. I found out by pure chance that certain types of music interfere with the functioning of the machine, during one of the missions in which my target was addicted to Elvis. His voice jams the machine, just like Beethoven disrupts other functions that they use to inhibit my freedom."

I turned to Milt and was happy to see him standing by the jukebox. "Keep it flowing, Milt," I said, and Milt nodded and kept pushing buttons.

"After many months of captivity I started to despair that I would ever be rescued. I have also been forced to do things that revolted me, so I worked myself into a coma and that's how I have been for the past month. They don't know what happened to me and they understand that I'm not faking it, but I'm too precious for them to give me up."

"So you're in a self-induced coma, but that's only toward the outside world and you can still make mice appear where you want?"

"That's right. I had to make them think that I had gone crazy or something, and at the same time I had to alert my people and hopefully get rescued by them. The problem was that I had to find an appropriate way to make contact with my unit without arousing suspicion, so I created a few random apparitions of mice, keeping in mind that they were following me and hearing what was said by and to them. And then I discovered that my cousin was doing an undercover job with Frankie Leone and decided to use him to get her attention."

"Your cousin Fairy?"

"I don't know what you mean by 'Fairy.' My cousin's name is Melissa."

"Whatever." I felt stupid; of course she wouldn't tell me her real name. "But why didn't you go straight to your cousin?"

"I was afraid that I might blow her cover. I didn't know how much the people who hold me would be able to learn from my movements. And besides, until you played Beethoven at me I wasn't able to speak freely, so going to her would have done me no good. No, the best I could do was to make myself conspicuous so Melissa would know that it was me and would find a way to get in touch with me."

"But you overestimated her. So far besides giving me a headache she has accomplished nothing. I think you're better off without her help. And I, on the other hand, am stuck with you."

"How's that?"

"For an ectoplasm-creating medium you're not too smart," I said. I was happy to be able to dial her self-satisfaction down a notch. "The bad guys—whoever they are—know that I have you, so as long as they don't get you back, they'll be after me, and you've seen what that means. Under other circumstances I would gladly give you to them, but they've pissed me off and there will be hell to pay when Lizzy sees her kitchen, so I'll have to stick with you and get us out of this mess."

"So that's where we stand. I'm a piece of meat lying on a bed in a basement and the bad guys know that you have played Beethoven at me and that I'm out of control, so they need to get hold of me—I mean the mouse—and destroy it before it can lead anybody to them."

"But wouldn't you just make a new one if this one gets destroyed?"

"They know I can't. One of the functions of the machine is that it can interfere with my ability to make mice, and I haven't found out the right music to neutralize that function yet. As soon as they understood that I had a plan of sorts and found out where I was, they turned that function on and now I'm stuck with this one mouse."

"Okay. You said that you know who can lead us to the basement, right?"

"I think so."

"So let's go and get you out of there."

"Would you do that for me?"

"Yeah, I don't like people shooting and throwing grenades at me."

"You may want to get in touch with Melissa first."

"We have no time to lose, but let's keep that in mind for later. How good is she?"

"Oh, she's good. Very good."

"I'll keep her in mind," I said again. I did have an open account with her and her Mickey Finn, but that would have to wait.

"Milt!" I called and he graciously cut off the phone call that he was making and approached. "I need your advice," I added.

"Sure, shoot."

"Without getting into too many details, I need to break into a basement that is probably heavily guarded by armed goons. I'll need some machinery and quickly."

"No problem. You can help yourself to my private collection. Let's go down to the cellar and I'll fix you up. You stay here," he said, addressing the mouse, "and come to get us if anybody tries to get in."

The mouse nodded in assent and I followed Milt to the back and down the stairs that led to the cellar. I had been there with him a couple of times, and I knew that his private collection included everything from a bazooka to a tiny pistol that you could hide in your inner pocket. I was sure that I would find what I needed there. The stairs ended before two heavy metal doors, and I went to the one on the right-hand side.

"No," said Milt, "the left one."

"I thought that you kept your stuff in here."

"I did, but then I added a lot to my collection and there wasn't enough room, so I had to move it. Here, take a look," he said as he opened the door. "The light switch is on the right."

I stepped in, feeling the wall for the switch, and as soon as I found it and switched on the lights, the door closed behind me and I heard the lock turning. I ran to the door and banged on it. I opened the small spy window of the door and saw that Milt was standing outside.

"What's the matter, Milt? What game are you playing at?"

"Sorry Dave. Just business. While you were having your chat with that mouse I got a phone call from a very good client of mine—one to whom I can never say no. He called me to commission a very simple job: I was to bring to him one white mouse, which by mere coincidence is the one that you brought here."

"You treacherous son of a bitch!"

"Don't take it too hard, Dave. I'm doing you a favor. If you walked out of the door with that mouse on your person your life wouldn't be worth a cent. This way I'm saving you and making some money; it couldn't be fairer than that."

"Your mother did the night shift on the pier and made you with a syphilitic midget," I threw at him. I remembered how sensitive he was about his low stature.

"I understand that you're angry right now, but after you calm down you'll see that I acted sensibly. I'll come back to let you out as soon as I can. Meanwhile, you'll find food and booze inside. You can stretch out on the bed on your left. Don't wait up; it can take me some time to conclude this transaction."

He started to climb up the stairs but stopped when I called. "Wait! Who is your client?"

"Dave, Dave ... You surprise me ... and shock me. You know very well that I can't tell you that—crook-client privilege," he said, shaking his head sorrowfully. "And oh, don't worry about Jake, he's harmless," he added, and with a wave of the hand he disappeared from view up the stairs.

CHAPTER 7

I turned around, ready to face the danger. I wasn't buying Milt's statement that Jake—whatever it was—was harmless. I knew Milt's distorted sense of humor, and I expected it to be a blood-thirsty Doberman or some other similarly deadly creature. Luckily, I still had my .38 with me and I drew it. That dog was in for a surprise.

Something stirred at the dark end of the long room and in spite of my weapon I felt a shiver running up my spine.

"Don't shoot, Mate," said a voice with an Aussie accent, coming from the dark. "Or you can shoot, if you like, but it won't do you any good. I'm coming out so you can see me."

A figure stepped into the light and I'll be damned if he didn't look just like Popeye the Sailor, complete with root pipe and all. He did look harmless, particularly since he was translucent, and I knew from experience that translucent ghosts can't harm you physically. I gaped at him; Milt never told me that he was keeping a ghost in his cellar.

"What's the matter, the cat took your tongue?" the apparition asked.

"Sorry, but you gave me quite a jolt. I was expecting something else." I pocketed my gun to improve the atmosphere and continued. "Who are you? How long have you been here?"

"I'm Jake, like your friend told you, and I've been here for the best part of the last two hundred years. It's not a bad place to be, but I get bored so I'm glad you're here; it's been a while ..."

I had to think fast. This could be my chance but I had to be careful—ghosts may be touchy at times and you have to know how to talk to them or they become uncooperative and it may take you ages to fix your relationship with them.

"I'm glad to meet you, Jake. I am Dave," I said, smiling my best smile, "and I'm happy to chat with you and relieve some of your boredom. I was wondering ... but no, I shouldn't be bothering you with my personal problems."

"No, no, speak up. Don't be shy, Mate."

"You see, I know that people in your condition like to stay put and don't leave the house much, but I'm in a fix here, and I was wondering if you could help me out."

"How?"

"You see, I'm locked in and I need to get out immediately or someone is going to be in big trouble. So I'd appreciate it very much if you could, you know, take advantage of your incorporeal situation to go out and get help for me."

Now that I had it out in the open I wondered how he would react. I watched his face closely and what I saw was sadness, not rage, and that was a good start.

"I'd be happy to, but unfortunately I have a little problem. It has to do with a Jamaican lady and some voodoo stuff that we don't need to go into, but the matter is, I can't leave the house unaccompanied. I can't go a hundred feet from this room, unless I get attached to a living person and then the one hundred feet rule applies to that person. That's my curse. You see, this building has been abandoned for decades, and when your friend Milt bought it I hoped that he would agree to help me, but he laughed at me and said, 'Do you really think that I would be seen in public with someone like you?' No matter how much I pleaded with him, he just kept laughing. That's your friend Milt."

"I don't know why you keep referring to him as my 'friend'. He's nothing of the sort. He just locked me in here and stole my property."

"Yeah, that's Milt all right."

"So what you're saying is that I'm stuck here until God knows when." I felt suddenly disheartened, something that seldom happens to me.

"Of course, if you're ashamed to be seen in public with me, that's it. Your choice, Mate."

"What do you mean, 'my choice'? When was I given a choice?"

"Boy, aren't you thick! I just told you that I can get out if someone accompanies me."

"I'd be ecstatic to accompany you out, but I can't walk through walls; I thought you realized that."

"Who's talking about walking through walls? Come over here and push this bed aside. You see this lid over here? Lift it up."

I did as instructed and a whiff of stale air hit my nostrils. All I could see was a pitch-dark hole with some steps apparently leading down into it. I looked at Jake, waiting for some more information.

"This shaft takes you into an underground maze that runs in five different directions," he explained. "Four of those routes take you to sure death—so horrid that nobody will ever find your bones. The fifth lands you on the fishing pier a mile from here. Get going."

"Are you nuts? Do you want me to take an eighty percent chance of getting killed? No thank you, sir."

"That's where I come in. I know the way and I can take you out. The price is that wherever you go, I go with you, at least for a while, and then you'll have to bring me back here when you're ready to split. Deal?"

The sudden vision of renewed freedom made me optimistic again.

"Deal! Let's go," I said with enthusiasm.

"Take this oil lamp with you. I don't need it, but it's pitch dark in there and I don't want you to slip and break your neck down there. The place is smelly and humid, so nobody ever comes down there and I'd hate to be trapped underground forever, forced to watch as your body slowly decays—"

"Okay! All right. I get the picture. I don't need the fine details. You lead," I said, and then I started lowering myself into the shaft after him.

I like to think that I'm courageous. I'm certainly not a coward, but that walk underground almost made me piss in my pants. It wasn't the spooky atmosphere with the wailing sounds, the strangely shaped shadows of contorted moving bodies, or things that looked like human body parts that I had to kick out of my way. It was when Jake suddenly stopped midway.

"What did you stop for?" I asked. Saying that I was anxious to get out would be a gross understatement.

"It's this junction. I'm not sure which way to turn."

"You're not sure? YOU'RE NOT SURE?! How can you not be sure? You told me you knew the way, didn't you?"

"Well, yes, I did, and I was sure I remembered it, but try being stuck in a basement for two hundred years and then tell me if your memory isn't a bit rusty."

"So what do we do now?" I'm not ashamed to say that at that point I was panicking.

"I'm almost sure that we need to turn right. Almost sure."

"I'm going to die," I lamented.

"Wait!"

We were walking a narrow path beside a canal of smelly water and Jake's attention turned to a wood slab floating in it. On the slab a distorted figure was curled up in such a way that I couldn't make out if it was a human being. Jake addressed him without hesitation.

"Hey, Mate. Can you tell me which way to the fishing pier?"

"The fishing pier? You see this junction here with the bridge over the canal? You need to turn right onto it and then go straight all the way to the fishing pier."

"Much obliged, Mate," said Jake, and the figure waved to him in response before disappearing into the darkness of the canal.

"We're going left," said Jake.

"But he said right," I objected. "I distinctly heard him saying that we should turn right."

"That's why we're going left," Jake explained patiently. "He's one of the scavengers who feed on the bodies of those who get killed taking the wrong way. We're turning left."

"You're a charming lot around here," I muttered, but turned left after Jake. What other choice did I have?

CHAPTER 8

It took us another 10 minutes to find a shaft with steps on which we could climb to get out, and after doing some pushing on an iron lid that was cemented to its base by dirt, we found ourselves on the fishing pier, not a moment too soon. The lighting was poor and the smell was only marginally better than in the underground world, and I soon realized that I was the carrier of that smell. Large stains decorated my suit and emanated foul odors.

"I need to get a shower and change," I told Jake. Since I was stuck with him I realized that I might as well fill him in on my plans.

"Sometimes we didn't shower for weeks on the boat, Mate. You don't need to go shower on account of a little grime. You want to go and find Milt and kick his ass, don't you?"

"Thank you for your moral support and your inspirational tales of filth. I'm going to take a shower now, and you can come with me or wait for me. Do as you please."

"As if I had a choice," said Jake, speaking morosely.

"We need wheels, and these will do," I said. We had walked away from the pier and were lucky enough to find a motorbike that was not locked up. It was parked outside a bar, and I hoped that its owner would be busy inside, drinking his head off. To cut the wires of the starter's key and to kick the engine alive was the matter of a minute. I jumped on the bike and gazed at Jake. He was clearly puzzled.

"What is that thing?"

"It's a motorbike, hop on," I ordered, and he simply nodded and seated himself behind me, just in time for me to drive away and to avoid the need to give awkward explanations to the little crowd that came running out of the bar.

It is amazing what a shower can do for you. Coming out of mine I felt another man altogether and my self-confidence grew a further notch after donning a clean suit. I had left Jake in the living room and that's where I found him. He looked pensive and kept quiet, which was okay with me. I wasn't in a chatty mood either.

"What now?" he asked, at last.

"Now we need to track Milt down. I think we'll start with his house; he thinks that I'm stuck in his cellar and has no reason to be careful. If he got careless and went home with the mouse, getting it back will be a piece of cake. Come with me."

"You don't have to tell me to come with you all the time. I can't get more than a hundred feet away from you, even if I wanted to," he reminded me.

"Okay, get in the car," I said, as we reached it. I took the driver's seat and he just walked through the door and sat beside me.

"You shouldn't do that when we have people around; it may elicit questions. I'll open the door for you next time, if we have company."

Jake nodded. He looked pensive and I wondered what was biting him. I drove slowly toward Milt's house because I didn't want to be stopped by a patrol while Jake was in the car. I'd have a hard time explaining him away. Not all ghosts are invisible to living people, and Jake was a ghost that everybody could see; walking around with him was awkward. When we finally reached Milt's street, I parked a few houses away and locked the car.

"We need to do some reconnaissance. Keep low," I ordered.

Milt's house was located in a quiet middle-class neighborhood, with well-kept lawns and freshly painted façades. The windows of his home were lighted and I circled toward the back, peeping through each window that I passed. The fourth window was where I got lucky. It was the kitchen window, a wide one just above the faucet; beside the sink I saw a small cage with my mouse in it. But when I say "lucky," of course I mean "spooked." Milt was not alone; the kitchen was a big one, but it seemed crammed on account of the four thugs who were playing cards and drinking beer at the kitchen table. The arsenal that they had dropped on the floor beside them would have made an army general very happy. There was absolutely no question of confronting them.

I lowered my head quickly and tiptoed away from the window. Jake, who until then had taken no interest in my doings, looked at me inquisitively.

"Milt is in there all right, but he's not alone. He has four dangerous-looking goons with him, complete with cannons and all. If I so much as show my face there, they'll blow it to pieces. I don't know what to do."

"In my time ..."

"Don't start telling me about your times, please. I need to think and your prattle gets in the way."

"All right, I'll keep quiet if you want, but I was just saying that if Milt has thugs with him, you should bring more thugs and bigger ones. It stands to reason."

I gazed at him in awe.

"You know what? I take it back, you're a genius. You just gave me an idea."

"I told you so. In my time ..."

"Don't push it, okay? Now keep quiet." We had moved sufficiently far away from the house that I felt comfortable making a phone call. I dialed a number I knew too well and waited anxiously for it to be answered. I never thought that Frankie's voice could sound beautiful to me, but this time it was music to my ears.

"Who's that?" he barked.

"It's me, Dave Callaghan."

"What's the matter with you? It's the bloody middle of the night. I didn't give you my personal number so you could wake me up whenever it pleases you."

"I'm sorry, Frankie, but this is really important. I wouldn't be disturbing you if it weren't important ... for you."

"It better be good. Much, much better be good. For you, I mean. Is it good?"

"Yes, it's good. Listen ..."

CHAPTER 9

You have to hand it to Frankie—where goons are concerned he has the best and most diverse collection this side of the river. It took him only a little over half an hour to deliver a good assortment to me, as promised. We had been waiting a few houses away, out of sight of Milt's home. I was worried, not the least because of Jake, who had turned mulish.

"Get behind those bushes there," I ordered him.

"Why?"

"Because. Just do it."

"And what if I don't?"

"You have to. I can't explain you to the baboons that are coming to help us out of this mess."

"You."

"Eh?"

"To help *you* out of your mess. I had my mess two hundred years ago and nobody was there to help me."

"Okay, to help me. All the same, get behind that damned bush!"

"I might not be what I am now if someone had been there to help me, but nobody cares ..." said Jake and seated himself moodily on the curb with his chin on his fist. It maddened me. The last thing I needed now was a moody ghost on my hands.

"I care about you," I lied.

"You really do?" said Jake, brightening up.

"Of course. You helped me and I'll help you."

"I'll hide behind the bushes, but when you go back to Milt's house I'll have to come after you. One hundred feet, remember?"

"Yeah, yeah. Get moving now, I hear the noise of cars coming."

Jake disappeared behind the bushes and a few seconds later three vans stopped beside me. The first one disgorged four goons, each one the size of my refrigerator, only taller. I knew the one who seemed to be the leader because he had lifted me out of bed with one hand the night I was "hired" by Frankie, so I approached him.

"Hi, Ben," I said, flashing my friendliest smile, which as it turned out was wasted on him since he kept his dull countenance. "You in charge?" I asked.

"Rrr," he answered. He was a loquacious character.

"What do you have in the other two vans?"

"Six men and gear."

"You have instructions, right?"

"Yes. Kill the ones you point out to me and go back to report."

"Good. Take your men and follow me. Wait!" I ordered. A Mercedes had just stopped behind the last van and Boris, Frankie's bodyguard, emerged from it. I walked up to him quickly. If Frankie had come in person to oversee the operation, things might get complicated for me.

"Hey, Boris," I said when I reached the car. "The boss here with you?"

Boris shook his head and thumbed toward the car, which I took as an order to approach it. When Frankie orders you to approach, you approach, and presto, so I opened the rear door and was in for a surprise.

"Mrs. Leone, what are you doing here? This is a dangerous place."

"Come in and close the door," Lena ordered and I obliged.

Finding myself close to the boss's wife made me nervous. Frankie wouldn't like it, I was sure. She smiled at me and I had a déjà vu.

"You're better looking when you're erect," she said, and then I knew for sure.

"Fairy! That's you, right?"

"Yes, mister detective. Only my name is ..."

"Melissa," we said in unison.

"Why ... what?" I tried to articulate a question, but my head felt like a beehive.

"Listen, I'd love to chat with you, but let's leave it for some other time, OK? I need that mouse well and alive ... functioning I mean—or whatever it does. Are we clear on that?"

"That's what this is all about. We are going to storm the place and rescue the mouse."

"Sure. And what do you think will be the first thing the ones inside do? They'll destroy the mouse. Unless they are complete morons, that is. You must make sure to get it out of there first thing."

"Yes, thank you for the tip from the backseat," I said, and I meant it to sting.

"Don't be stupid!" she bit back. "I can't blow my cover until this is over, although I'd rather be there taking care of Anne's mouse myself. Anyway, I'll be watching your back. Now get out, you've been alone with me for too long as it is."

I got out and started to leave, but then I remembered that I hadn't told her about Jake and at some point she may see him and freak out. I opened the door again and poked my head inside.

"If you see a ghostly figure that looks like Popeye the Sailor, pay no attention; he's my personal ghost and he's harmless," I said and slammed the door, leaving her to chew on this piece of information. I smiled all my way back to Ben; it was some satisfaction knowing that I had left her puzzled.

Frankie's men were an impressive bunch. All ten of them were now grouped before the first van, each carrying various fire pieces, some of which looked like real cannons. I got close and started to explain.

"We have five armed men in that house, and one—ahem, individual—that we need to rescue. Last time I checked, they were in the kitchen, in the back of the house. We want to draw them to the front so we can rescue the individual through the kitchen window. That has to be done subtly, okay?"

"No problem," said Ben and the others nodded in assent.

"All right, then. I'll go to the back of the house. Give me a minute and then make some noise in the front of the hose—knock on the door or something."

We walked quickly toward the house and I pointed it out to the crew. Ben stood before the house, in a thinking position; thinking must've hurt his head, judging from his expression. Then he lifted the tube that he was holding in his hands and pulled the trigger. The door was blown to pieces with a deafening explosion.

"I said 'subtly,' didn't I?" I cried in despair as automatic fire came from the house, and bullets whistled all around.

I ran toward the back of the house, leaving Ben and his baboons to shoot it out with their peers. I prayed all the way to the back that I would get there in time. It surprised and startled me, but I realized that I had developed feelings for that mouse.

CHAPTER 10

When I got to the kitchen window, I was relieved to see that the mouse was alive and well—or, at least, if not alive, it was still functioning. The bad news was that the cage was now on the kitchen table, well out of reach of the window. I had hoped to be able to break the window, grab the cage, and run away, but that was no longer a viable plan. Much more so since they had left one of the big goons to guard the back door. He had a nasty-looking machine gun under his armpit, but he would have been scary enough barehanded. I was stymied.

"Let me handle him for you," an unmistakable voice said in my left ear. I turned and gazed at Jake.

"I hate to tell you, but you are incorporeal and there is nothing you can do to that monster, there in the kitchen."

"Watch me," said Jake, and without further ado he passed through the wall and went to stand before the extra-extra-large assassin, who eyed him doubtfully.

"Who're you?" he asked, looking puzzled.

"I'm Jake and I've come to take you with me."

"Take me where?"

"Down."

"Down?"

"Yes, down to hell where you belong."

I kept a low profile to avoid being seen, but through the window that I had managed to slide open a crack, I was able to follow this exchange. The battle on the other side of the house appeared to be going on with deafening results and I could almost see the goon's brain working to decide on a course of action. Finally, he followed the one that befitted his instinct and dealt Jake a blow with his fist, which went through him with no result. Jake stood there, smiling and sucking on his eternal pipe.

"What the hell ..."

"The hell is right," said Jake, still smiling. "That's where I'm taking you. Come with me."

The goon gaped at him, tried to hit him again with the same result, and then turned and ran away. Jake turned to me and made a gesture with his hand, as if to say "See that it worked?"

I reached for a garden chair and smashed the window with it. With the chair I cleaned the glass from the frame and then climbed inside and grabbed the cage.

"You took your sweet time about it," said the mouse, speaking petulantly.

I had no breath for any repartee, so I simply climbed next to the kitchen sink, cut myself on the glass shards in more places than I could count, and jumped down and out of the house. Apparently Ben had lost his patience because at that moment I heard a couple of really big explosions and the whole house went up in flames. The machine gun fire hadn't stopped, though, and I kept running fast. I wanted no piece of it. As I ran toward the Mercedes the backdoor opened and Lena/Fairy/Melissa stepped out and opened the driver's door. A very stunned—though apparently alive—Boris came sliding out of the driver's seat.

"Quick, get in the driver's seat," Melissa ordered.

She took the cage from my hand, and I let her have it since I needed both hands to pull Boris farther away, after which I sat behind the wheel. She sat beside me in the passenger's seat, and I switched on the engine and drove away. Behind us Frankie's goons were still pumping lead at the house but I think they were doing it just for fun because nobody could have remained alive in that mess.

"Melissa!" came the delighted call from the cage.

"Anne, dear," said Melissa. "I'm so glad ... how are you holding up?"

"Not so hot, to tell you the truth. You need to get me out of here."

"Sorry to interrupt," I said, "but where are we going?"

"Pull over here," said Melissa. "We need to talk."

"I want to know it too," came Jake's voice from the back seat. That gave Melissa quite a jolt.

"Who ... what is that?"

"Oh, that's Jake. I told you about him. He's with me. He's my personal and friendly ghost, pay no attention to him."

"Pay no attention? What do you mean 'pay no attention'?" Jake protested. "For your information, young lady," he added, addressing Melissa, "I am the one who rescued this mouse here. I think I deserve some respect for that, don't I?"

"Yes, Jake, I'm sorry," I said. He had really got us out of that mess, and I had started to respect him.

"All right," said Melissa, "you'll explain this to me later so it makes some sense. But now we need to talk to Anne and plan ahead."

"We need to find a good place where we can listen to a few Elvis songs, first. Do you happen to know one?"

"As long as you can assure me that you've not gone off your rocker ..."

"I know what I'm doing," I said in a tone that left no room for arguments.

"He knows it," the mouse said.

"Who's this Elvis?" Jake asked, but nobody paid attention to him.

"All right, then start driving," said Melissa, "and I'll direct you to a safe place where we can all sit down and relax with some good music."

"Not just any music. Elvis," I said, and then I released the brake and drove away.

CHAPTER 11

"Stop here! Turn right inside," said Melissa.

"This car doesn't need washing," I pointed out to her. She had made me stop in front of an automatic car washing place.

"Drive straight through the tunnel and then turn left," she ordered, as if I hadn't spoken.

For want of a better idea I did as instructed but turning left was out of the question. "Left where?" I asked. "Do you want me to crash into the wall?"

"Exactly. Get going."

"You asked for it," I said, and pushed on the accelerator.

The wall turned out not to be a wall, after all, as it opened to let us through. It led into a neat parking space, and as the wall closed behind us, a man came out of a door and waved to us. I stopped the car and killed the engine. Melissa had already gotten out of the car and was standing beside it. The man approached us and peered into the car, and then he turned to her.

"Hi, M. What have we got here?"

Melissa smiled a broad, self-satisfied smile. "We have Anne back ... well, sort of."

The man poked his head into the car through the back window and stared at the cage. "Is that really you, A.?" he said.

"It is me, and what about letting me out of this thing here?"

"Oh, sorry, Dear! I should've let you out sooner, but as you know, we've been busy."

She opened the cage and stuck her hand inside. The mouse climbed it and settled itself on her shoulder.

"And what else do we have here," said the man, pointing his nose at me. I had started to dislike him already.

"This is Dave Callaghan and Mr. Jake, his personal ghost, or so I was led to believe."

"Dave Callaghan? You are *the* Dave Callaghan? I'm honored!"

He shook my hand warmly. How could I go on disliking him after that? By sheer willpower, of course. He was the sleaziest specimen I had met in a long time. I have always hated dandies, but this specimen, besides dressing like one, had had his nails done too. Disgusting. Still, one had to be civil.

"I don't know what you mean by that," I said, "but unless there is another Dave Callaghan who works as a private eye and is plagued by ghosts, ectoplasms, and zombies, who all seem to want his services, then that's me."

"You're too modest. Just as I would have expected of you. And Mr. Jake ...?"

"Mate, I'm not his or anybody else's anything. I'm here because I can't help it."

"Well," said the man, "we'll sort it all out later. Let's go inside. And, oh, by the way, my name is Jeff, and I run this place."

Passing through the door was like going into another world. Inside, the atmosphere was a mix between the Pentagon and a classy hotel. Desks with computers and communication equipment were dotted around, along with sofas and armchairs. Jeff directed us to a corner where black leather armchairs surrounded a tea table. "Let me get you something to drink," he said, and as he lifted two fingers a waiter—another dandy—approached us. I ordered scotch on the rocks and as soon as it came I gulped it down. I hadn't realized until then how much I needed it.

Having ordered and gotten in no time a second round of drinks, Jeff motioned to us to follow, which I did, taking the glass with me. We went into a spacious elevator that took us an undisclosed number of floors down and opened into a lighted corridor. Jake was nowhere in sight, which was fine with me, and Jeff, Melissa, the mouse, and I walked into a large meeting room with a fake window opening into a synthesized Alpine landscape. A stereo system was playing Elvis's version of Besame Mucho.

"Make yourself at home," said Jeff, apparently speaking to me.

"Look here," I said. "I'm starting to have enough of this story, so let's get busy, OK?"

"Sure," said Jeff, speaking conciliatorily. "We all want this operation to be concluded. Let me give you a few updates and then we can move on."

He had remained standing and now paced the room while speaking, which is something I find annoying. I did want to get on with it, however, so I bit my tongue and listened.

"First of all, kudos to Melissa for nailing down Frankie Leone and his organization. With all the evidence that she collected, our men have arrested him and fifty of his gang and we are confident that he will stay behind bars for many happy years to come."

He paused, perhaps waiting for a round of applause, and I turned to Melissa. Something had been weighing on my mind, and I wanted to ask her about it.

"How did you manage to survive being with that piece of cheese? I mean, I understand duty and all that rot, but being misses Frankie Leone ..."

"Does that bother you?" Melissa asked with a smile.

"Nooo. I'm asking just out of curiosity."

"Curiosity, I see ... well, Frankie only needed me as an ornament. He doesn't ... function, so to speak."

"You mean, he's impotent?"

"I guess. He made it quite clear to me at the outset that I shouldn't expect to get sex from him. He needed me for business events only. He wanted to parade me before his business associates and show them what a man he was. Pathetic, isn't it? We slept in separate rooms, which suited me fine."

"I see."

"All right. Enough with Frankie Leone. Let's get down to the main business!" said Jeff. "And the main item on the agenda is, where Anne is being kept and how we can get her out of there."

The mouse was on the table, turning its head from one speaker to the other as we spoke. But now silence fell on the room and she turned to me and gazed at me expectantly. I was as clueless as the others, but I recalled something she had said.

"You said to me that you don't know where you are kept, but you know who knows. Tell us who is that?"

"Well ... I know and I don't. What I was referring to, is that these guys—the ones who are keeping me—seem to live on pizza and they always buy it from the same place. The pizza delivery boy must know where that is."

"The pizza boy!" Jeff and I yelled in unison.

"Yes, the pizza boy."

"Do you know ... do you happen to have any idea of how many pizza places this city has? Thousands! Multiply that by the number of delivery boys for each pizza place and that gives the chances of finding your guy. Let's make a quick calculation," I said, cruelly, "and, yes, the chances are ZERO!"

"Calm down, Dave," said Melissa, and then turned to the mouse. "But, honey, there is something in what Dave says. Can't you remember some other detail that can help us?"

"Well, I remember that the box had a bull's head or something on it. I only saw the box once or twice and it was a long time ago..." The mouse's expression had become almost human and I felt sorry for it.

"Wait a second," said Melissa, suddenly excited. She went to a terminal at the end of the long conference table and started typing, but after a few seconds her excited expression disappeared and she looked up from the computer screen. "There is no 'Bull's Pizza' in this city. And I thought I had hit it ..."

I have flashes, when ideas come to me. That's why I can make a living as a detective. I had one there and then.

"Look up 'Bison Pizza,'" I said.

Everybody gazed at me and then, without a word, Melissa got busy at the keyboard.

"Here it is!" she cried out. "Bison Pizza. They have three branches. You're a genius, Dave!"

"Modesty apart, I must say that it takes some investigative power to ..."

"Oh, cut it out!" Melissa ordered. "Every minute counts. Let's get busy."

"I don't like bossy ladies, you know, but I happen to agree with you. Every minute counts," I said, and got up. "Give us some portable Elvis to play in the car. We may need to confer with Anne at some point."

Jeff nodded and spoke into the phone. "It will be waiting in the car for you," he said and hung up.

We all filed out of the room and waited by the elevator. The silence was broken by a high-pitched shriek, followed by a wet woman barely covered by a towel, who came out of a door with a "shower" sign on it.

"A man got into my shower. He came out of nowhere and was there," she sobbed at Jeff. She didn't wait for him to speak and ran on.

"Come out of there, Jake," I said, trying not to laugh.

Jake walked literally through the door and joined us. "Mate, I don't know why she made such a fuss. I've seen 'em more naked than that in my days."

"You ..." Jeff started to say, but I raised my hand and stopped him.

"Jake deserves some fun, after all. Anne wouldn't be here if it weren't for him," I said.

Jeff shook his head and pushed the elevator button furiously, but kept silent. Jake smiled at me and gave me a thumb up. I wasn't just being kind to Jake without a reason; I had the definite feeling that we would need his help soon and I wanted him in a good mood. Melissa grabbed my arm, and when I turned to her, she nodded in approval. That gal was smarter than I had thought at first.

CHAPTER 12

We stopped in front of the first Bison Pizza on our list and I turned on the tape recorder that Jeff had given me. Elvis's voice started singing "It's Now or Never."

"Is this the place, you reckon?" I asked the mouse.

"How would I know?" she answered. "I never was here. I may recognize the delivery boy because I saw him once caught on a surveillance camera, one day that they got careless and let me get near a screen, but that's all."

"I see ... I have an idea. Jump into my jacket pocket. I'll go inside and take a look around and you'll check the staff to see if anybody rings a bell, OK?"

"I can do that, but I won't talk to you while we are there, unless we can take Elvis with us."

"I don't think so. Just take a good look around and we'll come back here to talk. Melissa, you stay here with Jake—No, Jake! You can't come in," I wasn't letting him show himself around there.

"I wasn't saying that I was comin', but why not?" he complained.

"He's right, Jake," said Melissa, with her melodious and soothing voice. "It would be difficult to explain you to people in a crowded place. Besides, you wouldn't leave me here all alone, right? That wouldn't be gentlemanly of you."

"Oh, all right. But I get bored, so why don't you take your top off for me while they're gone?"

"You wish!"

"Dave?" he said, wistfully.

"No time for that now, Jake," I said and got out of the car before the discussion degenerated.

The pizza house was crowded and I moved around the place, turning so as to let the mouse peek at each and every employee, but each time after a long look it shook its head to signify that that was not him. Disheartened, I walked out and back to the car, only the car was not there, if you follow me. Jake was seated on the sidewalk, watching a cockroach with apparent interest.

"Where is the car?" I cried. "Where is Melissa?"

"I dunno. She didn't take off her top so I got out, to find something interesting to look at, like this roach here. Then a man came and got into the car and the car drove away. End of story."

"Who was the man? What did he look like?"

"How would I know? I wasn't looking."

"But, what about Melissa? Did she say anything?"

"Oh, sure she did."

"What did she say, then?"

"She said 'Ahhhhhh!' or something like that."

When Jake decided to be difficult he could be exasperating, but I knew that I had to keep asking him, to get answers.

"And what about the man? Did he say anything?"

"Oh, yeah. He said, 'Don't give me any trouble, M.', I think, or something like that."

"Dave ..." that was Anne, trying to attract my attention from my pocket.

"I know, Anne," I said, quickly silencing her. "We've lost the music, so I need you to go out of earshot. I want to talk to Jake."

"I understand, but I think I'm on to something ..."

"So am I, so am I. Now be a good girl and get the hell outa here so Jake and I can talk."

The mouse gazed at me pensively for a few seconds and then it climbed down and ran away. I watched it going until I was sure that it couldn't hear us and then I turned to Jake.

"Listen, Jake. You're a great guy, you know that?"

"Why ... sure, but why are you telling me that?"

"Because I need you to do something for me. I think that you'll be saving the day and that should be something for you to be proud of, seeing what a great guy you are."

Jake kept looking puzzled, and when he said nothing, I continued. "You see," I said, "I got a hunch ..."

"A what?"

"A hunch. That something that we detectives get sometimes. That's why we are going to go back to the car wash and I need you to do some scouting for me when we get there."

"But they took our car, so how are we going to get there?" Jake asked, and I was surprised that he was actually taking an interest in the process.

"The car wash is only six blocks away—that's part of the hunch—so we walk. And when we get there, I'll tell you what kind of scouting we need. Are you game?"

"I'm game, but on one condition?"

"Condition? What condition?" I didn't know that ghosts had conditions, but then he gave it to me and I understood. It made sense, sort of, knowing Jake as I did by then.

CHAPTER 13

I was so pissed off that I almost ran all the way back to the car wash. When we got there it was still dark and the streets were empty, which was great, seeing what an odd couple Jake and I made, not counting the mouse that had climbed back into my pocket. We started at the side of the building next to the entrance.

"Off you go," I told Jake.

"You remember the one hundred feet limit ..."

"I do. When you reach it come up and I'll move along the wall, and then we'll repeat. Now get going," I ordered, and Jake walked through the wall. I was always impressed seeing him do that, no matter how many times I had seen him do it before.

"Not here," Jake said, reemerging after a few seconds, and I moved along the wall an estimated hundred and fifty feet, to ensure that he was covering everything. As I stopped he walked through the wall again.

We repeated that routine several times until in the middle of the rear wall of the building Jake emerged, speaking urgently. "That section next to you is a concealed door. Grab it as it opens because if it closes again we're done for."

He dived in again and five seconds later the wall opened, revealing a concealed door, and a man shot out and ran into the street. By the time I grabbed the door and turned to see what had happened to him, he was gone. Jake's head popped out through the door.

"Are you coming in or not?" he asked.

"How did you do it?" I asked. I was genuinely surprised.

"A piece of cake. I met this guy in the corridor and he said, 'Who are you', and I said, 'Why are you wasting time? The police got in and are arresting everybody,' so he turned and ran to the escape door. That's when I popped up to warn you that it was going to open. Are you coming in or not?" he repeated.

"You're a genius, Jake!" I said as I walked through the door.

He sucked on his pipe, looking pleased, and I pulled my .38. I had to remind myself that we still were in danger.

We walked along the corridor and Jake popped in and out of closed doors, until he came out of one and said, "Your girl is in here."

"She's not my girl," I said through clenched teeth.

"Have it your own way," said Jake. "Anyways, she's alone and there is a key in this lock here, if you want to know. Go get her, you dummy!"

I turned the key in the lock and the door opened, revealing a much-shaken Melissa, who, God knows why, flung herself into my arms, murmuring, "Oh, Dave." I gave her a reassuring hug and then I pushed her away. She gazed at me and reassumed her composure. "The son of a bitch!" she said.

"You mean, Jeff, I presume?" I said.

"Jeff!"

She said it as if "Jeff" were a particularly disgusting and smelly piece of garbage. "He has made a nice little business for himself, using the basements as his own personal operation center. He has three operatives with him."

"Two, now," Jake corrected her.

"But how could he pull it off? This is a government facility. Why wasn't he found out?" I marveled.

"He is an Agatha Christie fan. He told me that the best place to hide something is under the nose of those who might be looking for it. Anne is in the room at the end of this corridor. He showed her to me."

We all ran out of the room and to the end of the corridor. I kicked the door and went in, gun first—a useless exercise because the room was empty but for a bed on which a girl lay—but I knew that it made me look good, so it wasn't a complete waste of energy, after all. The mouse ran out of my pocket and up the bed. It finally settled on the girl's chest and yelled, "Me, wake up!"

I turned to Jake and spoke urgently. "Keep guard in the corridor," I said. He nodded and disappeared.

Anne's limbs started to move and Melissa and I hastened to disconnect her from a variety of wires and tubes that were attached to her body. She opened her eyes and blinked. She was a rather plain woman, but in that moment she looked like the most beautiful creature on Earth, happy as I was to see the end of this nightmare. But of course it wasn't through yet.

"Two men coming," said Jake's voice in my ear, and my brain was kicked back into action.

"Lie down as before," I ordered Anne. "Melissa, you hide behind this equipment," I said, and I knew that I didn't need to tell a trained agent what to do next.

I hid behind the open door just in time for Jeff and another dandy to miss seeing me.

"What the hell ..." Jeff started to say, but I didn't let him finish. I came out from behind the door, gun first.

"Keep your hands above your head, if you want to keep having one!" I said, speaking menacingly.

Jeff and the dandy didn't argue, which wasn't surprising since arguing with a .38 is a fool's errand. Anne sat up and Melissa came out from behind the equipment and I enjoyed seeing the look on Jeff's face.

"This is all a big misunderstanding," Jeff started to say. "I am a government agent and you are trespassing on government premises and jeopardizing a delicate operation. I recommend that you stop interfering ... eeeyouch!"

The latter exclamation was due to Anne having kicked him hard in the left shin. He doubled with pain and then Melissa approached him and kicked his right shin. "And that's for pinching my bottom!" she explained calmly. Jeff fell onto the floor where he remained, whining in pain.

"Is there anybody else that we should worry about?" I asked Jeff's companion. "Be careful not to lie to me. I have no patience."

"No, no," said the terrorized dandy. "There are only four of us. One is away and one has disappeared. All the others in the building think that this is a top-secret operation. They know nothing of all this."

"Good," I said. "Turn around. Melissa," I added, "bring over some of those wires and tie him and your friend Jeff up."

Having tied them up the job seemed to be completed, so I turned to the crew, at last feeling relaxed and able to smile.

"This wraps it up, thank God. Melissa, I assume that you will be able to explain your friend Jeff to the high brass, so it seems that we can go up and then home."

"Ahem ..." the sound came from Jake and I turned to him. "The condition..." he prompted me.

"Oh, yes ... I had forgotten it. Ehm, Melissa ..."
"Yes?"

"You see, when you were kidnapped we all were very worried about you and felt that it was important to rescue you as quickly as possible. Then I asked Jake to do some scouting for me and he agreed—he didn't have to, as you know, with him being a ghost and all that—but he made a condition, which I had to accept ..."

"Yes?" said Melissa again, but this time she spoke more dangerously.

"So now it's time to ... you know ..."

"No, I don't."

"Take off your top for Jake," I murmured quickly.

Silence ensued and I waited for the explosion, which strangely came as Melissa burst out laughing. When she was done convulsing with laughter she turned to Jake and said, "Of course, Jake, I'll be happy to take my top off for you." She started removing her blouse and then she turned to me and said, "Out you go, Dave." My luck, of course.

CHAPTER 14

As expected, the Feds made a production of it. We were interrogated for hours, as were the car wash facility employees. The most interesting part of it was seeing a tall agent in an expensive business suit trying to get something out of Jake, who after a while clammed up and sat there sulking and sucking on his pipe. After a couple of hours the interrogations continued in separate rooms, after which we were brought to a conference room where another elegantly dressed agent waited to speak with us. We had been up and about in that place for some 18 hours and I was wasted. I sat next to Melissa and she leaned toward me.

"He's the Assistant Director. Important guy," she answered my unspoken question.

"Ladies and gentlemen," he started out, quite pompously, "our organization—no, our country—owes you a debt of gratitude for all you have done. We are still reviewing the information that we collected ..."

I'd had more than enough, so I got up.

"Does repaying that debt of gratitude include letting us go, and stopping bullshitting us?" I asked. "Yes?" I added, and seeing that the Big Shot was speechless I got up and said, "See you around," to the room, and walked out.

In the street I hailed a cab, got in with Jake in tow and gave my home address to the driver. Saying good night to Jake, taking a quick shower, and crashing on my mattress, was the work of five minutes.

I got up in the morning with Jake yelling in my ear, "Open the damn door!" I shook the mist of sleep away and heard the doorbell for the first time. My watch said 10 AM, which wasn't an unreasonable time to have visitors, so I grabbed my pants, put them on and opened the door. Melissa was on the mat.

"Good morning. Did I wake you up?"

"Yes, you did."

"May I come in all the same?" she asked, and I moved aside to make way for her.

In the living room she sat on the couch without waiting for an invitation. Jake sat beside her, fixing his gaze on her breasts, as if to savor the memory of the night before.

"I need coffee," I said. "Want some?"

When she shook her head I went to the bathroom to brush my teeth and then to the kitchen to make coffee. With a big mug of strong coffee in my hand I sat on the armchair in front of the couch and felt equal to talking.

"What are you doing here?" I asked.

"Thank you, I'm glad to see you too. I owe you ..."

"You owe me nothing," I said. I hate it when people feel obliged to me.

"I owe you," she insisted, "for rescuing me, so the least I can do is to give you some practical information. Do you want to hear it?"

I made a gesture with my mug, meaning "go ahead," and she continued.

"Your friend Milt is dead—more or less vaporized with his house."

"May his black soul burn in hell," I mumbled.

"That leaves an open issue with his pub. Headquarters are aware of Jake's peculiar situation and have been discussing ways to deal with it. Finally, since Milt had no living relatives, the building has become government property. The government has turned the ownership of the building over to you, if you agree, that is," she said, handing me an official-looking document.

I hadn't seen that coming. I wasn't sure that I had any use for the old building, but then I saw how Jake got up and leaned toward me, his face alight with excitement.

"Mate, that's amazing! I can stay in the pub and you can come to me for help whenever you like. We make a good team, don't we?"

I hadn't given any thought to the day after, but I must admit that Jake came in handy for some jobs, and I may want to use him again. But there were problems that we hadn't thought through.

"But Milt was running the pub. I won't be there and the place will be closed and will fall apart. Besides, you won't be any better off than before, staying there all alone."

"We have thought about that too. The Agency is closing down the car wash facility, which they feel has been compromised. If you agree to let the building to the government, they will turn it into the new facility, so they will run it and you won't have to worry. Jake will have company and will be able to amuse himself ... within limits. You won't be able to show yourself to real customers," she added, turning to Jake.

"Yes ... that would work," I said. Things were starting to fall into place. A sudden thought occurred to me. "What has happened to the mouse?" I asked.

"Anne has become so attached to it that, rather than reabsorbing it like she does with spent ectoplasms, she decided to keep it. It will keep Jake company and Anne will use it every now and then."

"You seem to have thought pretty much about everything," I said. I didn't know whether I should be happy or annoyed.

"Well ... almost. I have one more thing to take care of, but first why don't you take Jake back to the pub? Meanwhile I'll deal with the remaining issue. Can I wait here while you're gone?"

"No problem," I said. "Don't steal my spoons, though. They're a present from my late mother."

Returning Jake to the pub was an easy job but an emotional one. We drove to the dock in my car with Jake sitting next to me. Melissa had given me keys to the newly fitted lock that those maddeningly efficient Feds had put on the door. We went down to the cellar to close the lid to the underground, which had remained open since our escape, and then we went up again. At the door I stopped to say goodbye.

"You've been a good friend, Jake. I hope we'll work together again soon," I said, and I meant it.

"Mate, you're great. Really," he said, and made a hugging movement, which was unpleasant because it sent a few cold spikes through my body.

I took a step back, hoping that it would not offend him, and left. At the car I looked back to make sure that the 100 feet rule had switched back to the house, and, reassured that Jake was not in sight, I got into the car and drove back home.

When I let myself in, my apartment was really quiet. The atmosphere was weird; the living room was empty and the lights had been turned off, which immediately brought me to a state of alertness.

"Where are you?" I asked, backing into a corner to avoid being surprised by a potential attacker.

"I'm in the bedroom," came Melissa's voice.

"Are you alone?" I asked, still concerned.

"Yes."

"Come out of there slowly, so I can see you," I ordered. I had my .38 ready in my hand and wasn't going to take any nonsense.

A movement announced that someone was coming, and squinting through the semi-darkness I saw a body standing at the bedroom door, leaning against the doorframe. She could or could not have been Melissa, but I was taking no chances. My hand went behind my back where I knew that the main living room light switch was, and I turned on the lights.

It was Melissa all right. She wore the black tights and the gorgeous mask that she'd had on, that night at the Venetian. A pair of handcuffs were dangling from her hand.

"Are we going to take care of that unfinished business or not?" she asked, and without waiting for an answer she turned and disappeared into the bedroom.

I followed her. What else could I do?

EPISODE FOUR

THE ACCOUNTANT

CHAPTER 1

I had barely pushed the squeaky door halfway through when she appeared, as if she had been waiting by the entrance, and maybe that's what she was doing. She wouldn't have been unattractive—for an aging madam that is—if it weren't that someone had done an unclean job of slitting her throat and her head had a weird tilt to it. I gazed at her, waiting for a sign, trying to ignore Bertram's petulant complaints.

"Why are you stopping? Why don't you go in?" he whined into my back from the first step, where he had stopped so as not to ram into me.

"Hello, big man!" she said, smiling with lips that had too much smeared lipstick on them. "Welcome! Come in, come in."

"In a moment, ma'am," I said. I needed a pause to think.

"What is it? Who are you talking to?" Bertram kept nagging. He stuck out his neck as far as it would go to look around the door, but I knew that he would see nothing.

Some say that my ability to see dead people is a gift, others think of it as a curse. The jury is still out on that, but at least it helps me make a living. Working as a detective is a highly competitive job, and I need the edge that my deadies vision gives me. I know from experience that ghosts can't harm you, at least not directly, and when you realize that, it opens up a whole range of possibilities as a detective. You exploit your vision to get information instead of running for your life.

"I told you to stay home, Bertram. Now you should really go. For your safety."

"My safety? Why?" he asked, but he got off the steps leading to the decrepit house—a good start, as I was anxious to get rid of him and on with the job of searching the premises. I had plans for that evening—or at least, for the second part of it— and wanted to get back home in time for them, so I gave him a little final push.

"The thing you can't see would suck your soul into the house and then..." I left it hanging there, lifting an eyebrow to add mystery to the unspoken threat.

Bertram walked backwards to his car and fumbled for the door without shifting his gaze from me.

"I'd better be going, then, you think?" His voice trembled so much that I had a hard time hiding a sneer.

"Better. Much better," I agreed.

"I'll see you back at the office, then. When you have news," he said. He fiddled with the car keys as he spoke, trying to sound calm but missing the keyhole several times in a row. He finally found it, managed to open the door, jumped into the car and sped away, at last allowing me to get down to business. I turned my attention to the madam, who was waiting patiently on the mat.

"Miss," I said with my politest smile, "I'm looking for a customer of yours. May I come in?"

"Business has been slow, lately," she lamented, "and you are the first customer today. Let me take you to see the girls. I'm sure that you'll find one to your liking ... or two, perhaps," she added hopefully.

She moved aside. I nodded, stepped in and closed the door behind me.

I don't know why I agreed to take that job. Well, actually, I do know why. Bertram is a pain in the neck, but he is also one of the few regular customers I have, and he gives me straight work, by which I mean regular jobs involving living persons. He is a constructor and owns a large, profitable business. From time to time, he needs me to uncover petty thefts by his employees or to find a debtor who has disappeared. He knows, of course, of my special ability in pursuing paranormal cases, but until now he had never had a real one, if you don't count the time he had this fixed idea that his deceased mother-in-law was following him around. She wasn't. But this time he was in the soup. Randolph, his head accountant, had disappeared, leaving him without access to his bank accounts, which he had never bothered to learn to manage. Can you beat that for stupidity?

A phone call from the accountant, recorded on his boss's answering machine, went like this:

"Help! I'm in this house. I don't know where they took me to. I can't get out. There is no door out, only in. Please help!"

I had traced the call as coming from a ruined house in Marlborough Road that had been there, rotting for ages. City records have it that it hosted a brothel until the police shut it down some time at the turn of the 20th century and it was sold to a faceless corporation just a year ago. I told Bertram that I would investigate and get back to him, but no—his accountant was apparently too precious to him and he had insisted on coming along. Now he was probably peeing in his pants all the way home. If you're not used to the supernatural you shouldn't play with it. To me it's something that goes with the job. I've seen enough of it and nothing will surprise me anymore.

The madam led the way along a dusty corridor, into a foyer that could have used a bit more light than what was coming from the draped windows. Six scarcely dressed young women sat on red velvet couches and they all turned to me as I walked in.

"Girls," said the madam, speaking cheerfully, "we have a customer. Make yourselves desirable. I'll go back to the door to wait for the next one."

With that, she left me alone in the middle of the room. The girls stood up one by one and made inviting gestures ... or what I might have found inviting if I had met them before they all got shot. I looked from one to the other, trying to decide which one would be the best to talk to. I ruled out the first one who had no face and was too much of a strain to look at. She had been shot from behind and the result wasn't pretty. The next two were so full of holes that they could have competed with a Swiss cheese. The two farther away from where I was standing weren't taking too much interest in me; they were busy whispering and giggling to each other. That left the one in the middle. She had a pretty face and a nice figure. There was nothing wrong with her tits either, if you ignored the hole right between them. She was smiling at me coquettishly, so I approached her.

"What's your name?" I asked.

"You can call me Honey," she said. "They say I'm softer than silk. Come up with me and I'll show you why."

She started to move, but I checked her with a raised hand. "No so fast, Honey," I said. "A couple of questions, first."

"Questions? About what? If you're after the shooters, I know nothing. Those pigs came in and started shooting. That's all I know."

"Not about that. I'm looking for a customer of this honorable establishment. A recent one. A little squirt with thin, blond hair. Here, look at this picture," I said, pulling from my inner pocket the one that Bertram had given me. She didn't even look at it.

"We haven't had any customers for ages. You're the first."

"Listen, Babe," I said, losing some of my patience, "this guy has made a phone call from this house, so don't sell me any bullshit, 'cause I ain't buyin' it."

I strode to the small table by the wall on which stood an old-fashioned, massive black telephone. I picked up the receiver and turned the dial, but it stuck midway. The line was dead anyway. It had obviously not been used for ages. And it made sense, too. This joint had been shut down for decades so it stood to reason that it couldn't have a working phone line. Something was off.

"Yeah, I guess I was wrong," I murmured, and turned to leave, but she appeared before me as if to block my way.

"Wait!" she said. I could have walked right through her, of course, but something in her face told me that I should listen to what she had to say. Besides, walking through ghosts always gives me shivers, which is truly uncomfortable, and I hate it. She had buttoned her blouse, covering the hole in her chest and, paleness apart, she almost looked alive.

"Yes? Speak up," I demanded.

"I will, but not here," she whispered, turning her head to look back, as if to make sure that nobody was there to listen to us. "Follow me," she said at last. I appreciated the effort she put into going through all the walking motions—I don't like it when ghosts simply float effortlessly at my side. She left through the door, turned right toward a stairway and started to climb it.

I'll never learn. I should have walked away and the hell out of that house. Instead, I followed her up the stairs.

CHAPTER 2

I treaded gingerly on the rotting steps, trying not to fall and break my neck, until we reached the second floor. The smell of mice and of damp, decaying wood was strong, and I had to breathe in short gasps to keep from gagging. She walked ahead of me and stopped at the second door of a long line.

"Here," she said, making an inviting gesture.

I grabbed the handle and turned it. The door opened without effort and I walked into a room that by the standards of a couple of centuries ago was luxurious. Now the bed had a sagging mattress covered with a pink rag and the mirrors that covered the wall and ceiling were foggy with the stains of time. I waited for her to come in and then I closed the door behind her.

"I'm listening," I said.

"Why don't you make yourself comfortable?" she asked with an inviting smile. "Take off your jacket and sit on the bed."

"Cut it out!" I snapped. I was impatient to get the info and to walk the hell out of there. "Tell me what you know about this man," I demanded, showing her the photograph again.

"He was here all right," she said, assuming a serious countenance, "and I can help you to find him."

"Good, tell me."

"Not so fast. I have my terms."

"Terms? What terms?"

"You need to get me out of here. You must help me to leave. Once

I leave here, I'll help you to find him."

"I don't get you, Sister. If you want to leave, leave. What's keeping you here?"

"It's the contract. I signed a contract with Susan—that's the madam—and unless she releases me I can't leave. And she won't let me go. I've begged with her many times."

"But—and don't take this personally—you're dead, I'm sure you know that. And all legal contracts end when you die."

"Go tell Susan that. I tried to leave more than once, but I can only make it to the door, and then I'm stuck. I need help."

Her story had credibility. In fact, I had seen other cases of ghosts that were kept within boundaries by invisible chains. My friend Jake, who is the ghost of an Aussie sailor, is also one of those cases. You'll find the details of his problem elsewhere in the archives. In short, he can't leave the house unless he attaches himself to a living person, and I have to go and take him out for airings from time to time. Jake has become what you might call "my house ghost," after a former friend of mine locked me in his cellar ... but that's another story and I can tell it to you another time. I shouldn't go on rambling now.

"All right," I said. "Assuming that I can find a way to get you out, what assurance do I have that you can help me?"

"I can, believe me. This little freak, Randy he calls himself, got the hots for my friend Lynn, and they eloped together. He was here all right—many times before—and I know how to find him. I'm sure I can. I'm telling the truth!"

"Well, start by telling me your real name."

"I'm Jessie," she said after a brief hesitation, looking suddenly demure.

"Okay, Jessie. I'll leave now and will think of some way to get you out of here."

"No, wait!" she said, speaking urgently. "If you leave just like that she will smell a rat."

"I can smell a bunch of them," I pointed out. "This place stinks."

"Very funny. You know I have no sense of smell. And you know what I mean."

"Yeah. But why should I care what your madam thinks?"

"It may be dangerous. I sense danger."

I've been in this line of business for too long to make fun of premonitions coming from people on the other side, so I took it seriously.

"What do you suggest?"

"Well," she said, smiling coquettishly again, "since we're here, why don't you loosen up and let me take care of you."

I felt my hair raising on the nape of my neck.

"I appreciate the proposal," I said, trying to keep a calm countenance, "but first of all you are incorporeal, and then I'm really not in the mood, right now."

"Aha, but I can manifest myself in a more tangible manner, when I need to. Here, feel this," she said.

She placed her two hands on my cheeks. I've been touched by all kinds of manifestations in the past, and it has always been unpleasant (if you don't count a friendly ectoplasm named Daphne, about whom I think I told you before). To my surprise, this time I felt something else. It wasn't the sensation of the touch of a human hand; it was completely different, a kind of warm vibration. But what spooked me was that it was pleasant.

"All right. I can feel you, but no thanks," I said, taking a step back. "Let's put up an act for your madam and then I'll go."

She looked hurt but said nothing. She sat on the bed—which was weird in itself because part of her went right through the coverlet and the mattress—and opened her mouth. "Ah! Oh! Yes! . . . Yes!" she cried out loud. She repeated that a couple of times and then she stopped and gazed at me.

"Care to help a little?" she asked.

"Not really," I said. "I don't yell as a rule. I can make the bed springs squeak a bit, if that helps."

"Yeah, do that," she said, but she shook her head impatiently, as if to signal that my contribution wasn't worth much.

I made a few half-hearted sitting jumps on the bed but had to stop when the dust it raised got into my nostrils. She kept her sound effects on for a while longer and then she gave up.

"I guess we've done what we could," she said, "with me doing all the heavy lifting, as usual. Quite frankly, you're a bit of a washout," she added, speaking reproachfully. "You're kind of cute and we could do much better if we went for real ... no, ah? OK." She finally sounded resigned and I got up. "Now we can go back. You go first and pay Susan," she said.

"Pay her, for what?"

"You don't think that you can come in here and have sex for free. This is a serious establishment."

"But I didn't have sex," I pointed out.

"So? You want them to think that you did, don't you?"

"Mmm ..." I said and I got up and walked out before her crooked reasoning gave me a headache. I navigated the steps with caution and in the hall I breezed past the madam, feigning not to hear her demand for money, opened the entrance door and left. Only I didn't, if you know what I mean. Instead, I saw a few stars when the blackjack hit me on the side of the head, and then I went peacefully to sleep.

I don't know for how long I was out but probably only for a few minutes. When I came to, my wallet was beside me, open and empty, with a scribbled note sticking out of it that said, "Next time pay for services." I had three hundred dollars in it and they were gone. They would go on the expense account, so that wasn't my loss, but I was pissed off because of the way in which I had fallen into a trap like a tenderfoot. I was also mad at myself for not listening to Jessie. I should have paid the madam. I knew who had hit me: Bugsy Malone. I had got a glimpse of him before blacking out. I knew him; he had been meddling with the occult before, and so had his father, but this time he was obviously connected to a ghost house and the implications required some careful thinking.

Bugsy was bad news. He had interests in the meat trade all over the city and if it was him behind this brothel, I would have to be extra careful. With Bugsy around it wasn't just a matter of dealing with ghosts. He was flesh and blood, and hot blood at that.

I walked away massaging my head. With the luck I was having that day, I had to walk ten blocks to find a cab.

CHAPTER 3

They say that time flies when you're having fun. Well, it flies also when you're getting your ass kicked. It was almost 6 PM by the time I got home, which meant that I'd been in that dump for almost four hours. My estimate was only 45 minutes chatting with the deadies. That pat on the head couldn't have knocked me out for more than 15 minutes, so what the clock was saying didn't square out. But I had no time to chew on it because I had to be ready to meet with Dolores (Dolly to her friends) at 7:30 PM on the dot, at the opera house. Not that I was looking forward to it, mind you, but I had no choice.

Dolly is my current girlfriend, if you care to call her that. We haven't put a label to it, but seeing that I am spending more time in the sack with her than with any other friend of mine, I guess it's reasonable to say that we are going steady. I still see my ex, Lizzy, and get to spend some time with her because I really like her and she still has the hots for me, but where animal passion is involved there is nobody like Dolly. That's why I put up with her weird demands, like this opera thing.

That's something I will never understand—how come that all my girlfriends have this passion for culture. My idea of a cultural night is a good game of poker or a boxing match but no—my girlfriends want to take me to museums and to poetry binges. It feels like I'm cursed and perhaps I am. When you deal with the occult, you never know on whose toes you may have inadvertently stepped, and that's exactly the kind of curse that one of my bitter enemies could have thought up for me.

Lizzy—Elizabeth to you—is a guide at the museum of modern art and in her time she made me see and read much more artsy stuff than I thought I could digest. She sort of dumped me because I refused to get what she calls "a steady job," one that would put me behind a desk for eight hours a day and probably kill me with boredom before I'm fifty. Dolly doesn't mind my line of work, but insists on taking me to fringe plays and musicals, which has now escalated into a fully blown opera. They were giving *Madame Butterfly*, that evening, which she insisted I would enjoy, although she must have known that I would be miserable from the get-go to curtains down. But if going through that kind of ordeal was key to taking her home afterwards, I was going to bite the bullet.

As soon as I got home, I undressed and jumped into the shower. The smell of the mice and of the rotten wood had stuck to my nostrils and I needed some steam to clear it out, so I turned on the hot water until a nice, hot fog filled the air around me. You could have knocked me down with a toothpick when that thin fog took shape. I have had all kinds of manifestations in my life, but having apparitions invading my shower was a bit too much, even for me.

"Daaave ..." the apparition wailed. "Heeelp meee. I am prisoneeeer."

I took a good look at him and I was damned if I could make out a face. I used my sleuthing instinct to conclude that it had to be the accountant.

"Randolph, is that you?" I inquired, to make sure.

"Yeees."

"Are you alive?"

"Yeees."

"Where are you?"

"Dunnoooo," was the answer, and then he disappeared.

Well, I'm asking you. How stupid can someone be? If you plan to invade the privacy of my shower at some point in your life (or death, for that matter), at least bring some useful information. Not like this moron, who besides giving me a jolt had accomplished nothing. He could have saved himself and me the trouble. But at least I had learned one thing: he was being held against his wishes, which could help me rule out some lines of inquiry that I had been considering. However, if he was alive as he had confirmed, how did he manage to project himself into my shower mist? This case was starting to become a bigger headache than I had expected.

I toweled up and dressed in my best evening suit. I am not a dandy, but I like to dress well and I know I look good when I'm groomed. Besides, showing off by taking a hot chick like Dolly around, is demanding. After all, *noblesse oblige*, like them Canadians used to say.

Knowing from experience that parking in the theatre district is next to impossible and then some, I took a cab and managed to get my nose under the wire just as Dolly was starting to look at her watch and to stamp the pavement outside the theatre. I barely made it before fire started to come out of her nostrils.

The performance was worse than I had anticipated. Stop me if you've heard this before, but it is all about this Japanese chick, who marries this American dude, who in turn disappears. When he comes back—and throughout the performance—there is a lot of weeping and wailing that goes on until, at last, the Japanese chick cuts her own throat and they let the audience go home. I slept through some of it and soon lost track of the plot, if there was one. That allowed me to concentrate on my current problem of how to get Jessie out of the whorehouse. I made no progress, but it helped me pass the time. Dolly was totally absorbed in the performance and ignored me most of the time, which was fine with me. At one point she jabbed me in the ribs with her elbow, and I saw that her eyes were damp.

"Poor girl," she whispered. "So tragic, don't you think?"

"Oh, ah," I said, trying to sound interested. She gave me a dirty look and went back to ignoring me for the rest of the performance.

Once we got outside I felt optimistic again. The ordeal was over.

"What do you say, Dolly, that we go and get a bite to eat first? Or shall we go straight to my place?"

"No, sorry. I don't feel like it. That was so sad ..."

"All the more reason to go and make merry," I explained.

"I don't think that I can be in the mood, tonight. I'm feeling blue. Please, let's take a cab and drop me at home, okay?"

That's what you get for being accommodating and going places not fit for humans. I'm sure now: I'm straight up cursed.

Since the evening was a washout I decided to try to do something useful, so after dropping Dolly off at home I went to my office and turned on my PC. Looking online for the shootout at the whorehouse didn't turn up much. All I found was a one-line mention in a historic web site, that said, "The multiple murder at the Marlborough Road house of ill-repute left 8 dead." I had counted six whores plus the madam, and including the one who had gotten away with the accountant it made eight. It checked out.

All of a sudden it hit me that Jessica had said that the accountant had eloped with her friend Lynn. But if the madam was holding the girls hostage with their contract, how come that Lynn was able to escape? And how—and why—does a ghost elope with a living person? Something in this picture was terribly wrong. I needed help to figure it out.

CHAPTER 4

I hadn't been down to the pier to see Jake for a couple of months, and I was a little ashamed to admit that I was only coming because I needed help. Besides, Jake is touchy sometimes, and may be mulish if he feels offended. I hoped he was in a good mood.

Let me tell you a little about Jake. I sort of inherited him while working on a case that brought me to the pub owned by my friend and mentor, Milt, who turned out to be a treacherous son of a bitch who almost got me killed. The pub was located in an ancient building on the pier, and Jake was a ghost that came with the property. He had been confined to that building for something like two hundred years, on the force of a curse placed on him. I never got the full details of the curse, but Jake says that it has to do with a Jamaican woman and some voodoo stuff that he would rather not talk about. Be that as it may, Jake is confined to that building. He can't go more than a hundred feet from it, unless he gets attached to a living person, and then the one hundred feet rule applies to that person.

At the end of the case that I was mentioning I got ownership of the building, which I lent to the government and is now used as a secret base for federal work—too complex a story to tell you about here, but you'll find it elsewhere in the archives. Anyway, along with the building I inherited Jake, who by then had become a dear friend, so when I can make the time I go and sit with him or take him out for an airing, to alleviate his boredom. This time, as always, he was delighted to see me. The place was empty except for the barman, who was a Fed I knew only to say hello to, and when I walked in Jake was yelling at him to change the song that was playing on the jukebox. He cheesed it courteously when he saw me.

"Mate! Great to see you. I was wondering what had become of you and was starting to get worried. I never know when someone may blow you to pieces."

"Great to see you too, Jake. How've you been?"

"Can't complain. You know they fitted the rooms downstairs with a new shower and I got myself a nice observation point in the ventilation shaft. This government agency here, they brought a couple of great-looking gals to work shifts downstairs. Great tits. It helps me pass the time."

"Glad to see that you keep yourself busy, Jake. I was thinking about taking you to work with me on a case if you're not too busy right now; what do you say?"

"Do you need to ask? I'm bored stiff trying to talk to that sorry excuse for a barman. Do you know that he was trying to make a Cuba Libre using gin instead of rum? And explaining it to him is like talking to that lamp over there. I'd be happy to get away from him for a while. What's the deal?"

"Not here. The walls have ears and I'd rather keep this private. I'll tell you later."

I got up and with a curt nod to the barman, I left with Jake in tow.

By the time we reached the Marlborough Road house I had brought Jake up to speed.

"A whorehouse, hmm," he said. "I haven't been to one of those for more than a couple hundred years." He had a smile on his lips and the dazzled look that I'd seen on him before, when he was contemplating convincing another friend of mine to take her top off in return for a favor she was asking of him. I didn't want him to be sidetracked into forgetting our job so I spoke to him severely.

"We're not going there for fun, you know? This is strictly business."

"I know, I know."

"Then please try to keep it in mind. We need to find a way to get Jessie out of there. Without her my investigation is stuck."

"Leave everything to me. Don't worry."

When Jake says that, it's when I really start to worry. But I said nothing. It wasn't the right moment to hurt his feelings. I don't know where a ghost gets off being touchy anyway, but I wasn't going to question it in the middle of an operation, so I just leaned against the wall and gestured him to get in. Jake disappeared through the wall and I stood there, waiting. I've seen him do it before, but it feels weird every time. Five minutes later Jake's head popped out of the bricks.

"I'm still tied to you and I can't get far enough inside. Start circling the house slowly, until I tell you to stop."

This hundred feet curse is really getting on my nerves. I must find some way to rescind it, when I get around to it. Right then I had little choice but to start walking along the walls of the house as Jake had asked me to, so I moved on.

"Stop!" came the order after a while, and then silence.

I had stopped under a shattered window and I heard voices coming from above. Then, Jessie's and Jake's head showed up in the window frame.

"Hi!" she said. "You came back for me ..."

"Yes, yes, I told you I would. Be quiet now," I silenced her. "What did you find, Jake?"

"This chick here, she's tied to the place all right. She wasn't kidding you."

"I understand that," I said, trying to hide my annoyance at being told things I knew already, "so how do we get her out?"

"We don't."

"We don't?"

"No."

"You're being very helpful," I said, bitterly.

"Unless ..."

"Unless what?"

"Unless I take her place while she's gone."

"How can you do that? You don't have a contract with the madam."

Sometimes Jake can be too condescending for me to bear. This was one of those times and what irked me was that he was clearly enjoying himself.

"Oh, it's too complicated to explain to you," he said. "You wouldn't understand. Let's say that there must be the right count of presences in the house, and I can be one of them."

"Will you do it? That's a lot to ask of you. You may be stranded here for a long time while I work to solve this problem."

"Let me ask you this: where would you prefer to be stranded, in a smelly pub with a half-witted barman, or in a whorehouse?"

"If you put it like that, I get you. Thanks. I'll come back for you as soon as possible. Hop down, Jessie," I added, turning to her.

Before I could bat an eyelid there she was, beside me. "Awesome!" she said, smiling broadly.

"Let's go," I said, turning to leave, but stopped when Jake called me from the window. I turned around and saw that he had two of the girls standing beside him, really close.

"Dave," said Jake, "don't feel obliged to come back too soon. I can rough it here."

I didn't need the smug smile on his face to figure that out. I waved in assent and strode away.

CHAPTER 5

Back at the apartment, I fixed myself a drink and sat in my best armchair in the semi-darkness of my living room. Jessie sat—if sitting is the right word for a ghost—on the armrest of the one next to me.

"Nice place you have here," she said after a long silence, speaking with open appreciation.

"Yeah," I said, and gulped down my pricey scotch, a gift from a happy client. I seldom turn to the bottle for encouragement, but at that point I needed all the boost I could get.

"Do you live here on your own?" she asked after a brief pause.

"Will you shut your trap for a moment?" I said, too worried to be polite. "I need to think."

"Oh, okay. You could be a little nicer to a lady, though," she retorted, sounding hurt.

My head was a beehive. There was enough there to worry anybody. For one, I had gone to all the trouble of getting Jessie out of the whorehouse and now I wasn't sure that she would stick with me all the way through and had to find a way to keep her working with me. Who knew if trusting her and taking Jake out of circulation was going to pay off? And then, what did she know that could help me and how was I going to get it from her, wasn't a simple question. Ghosts can be touchy, but also treacherous. I have known ghosts to play games with me just for the fun of seeing me squirm and run in circles. I had to be extra careful with her to avoid funny play, more so since she wasn't the ghost of Florence Nightingale or some other decent chick. Not that I have anything against prostitutes, mind you, but as a rule they are not particularly trustworthy. I had used up the only leverage I had on her and I needed information from her, which had better be useful.

"What do you know about Bugsy Malone?" I asked point blank.

"I know that he owns the building, our building, and is in business with Susan."

"How?"

"He sends her customers and gets the money she is paid for our services. He found out that once you are inside the house, you can see us and he's making a pile by sending healthy thrill-seekers to us."

"That's what I don't understand. Your madam has no use for the money, so why is she bothering?"

"Why are you bothering to breathe? For the same reason. He threatens to tear the building down and to turn it into a commercial mall. If he does it, our establishment will cease to exist, Susan will lose her status and will be relegated to either haunting the place or disappearing into nothingness. It's the same for the rest of us."

"So you have an interest in keeping Malone happy too," I pointed out.

For the first time since I met her, the smile on her face faded and she turned all serious.

"Have I? Can't you see farther than your nose, Mister Detective? Do you really think that I *want* to be stuck in that whorehouse forever? If the building is torn down and I can finally stop hanging around, I'll be happy to disappear and never come back again."

She had a tormented look on her face that made what she said sound real and meant. And it made me feel stupid for not realizing it by myself.

"I hear you," I said finally. "Now that I have freed you from the place you can disappear. There is nothing to keep you. Why don't you?"

She looked away and kept her gaze away while she spoke.

"That's what you think of me? That I wouldn't keep my promise to help you? That I would let you down?"

"The thought has crossed my mind," I admitted.

"Then you're more stupid than I thought, David Callaghan!"

She spoke with such intensity that she left me speechless. My glass was empty, pretty much like my head, when she spoke again.

"Aren't we going to go and find your accountant?"

"Sure we are. As soon as I can think of our next move."

"But, isn't that why you took me along? I can tell you what the next move should be."

"You can?" She got my attention there.

"I told you so."

"Okay, let's have it," I said, trying not to sound too eager.

She got up and came closer. "There is time for that. You're tense. Why don't you let me help you to relax a bit? If we are going to be partners, shouldn't we get better acquainted?"

In the semi-darkness she looked corporeal and rather nice. So much so that, for a moment, I forgot that she was dead. Luckily, when she sat on my lap I got the goosebumps that always result from my bumping into a ghost and I shook my impure thoughts away.

"I appreciate the sentiment," I said, "but we have work to do and I never mix work and pleasure. That's a rule I never break."

"Oh, you men! You're so boring," she said, jumping up.

"Sorry about that, but that's how it is. Let's talk about that next move."

"That's obvious. What kind of detective are you? We should talk to Inspector Pratchet."

"Who the hell is Inspector Pratchet?" I asked. I'd never heard of the man.

"Come with me and I'll show you," she said, heading for the door.

CHAPTER 6

My work often takes me to filthy, Godforsaken dumps, but this one was possibly the worst I'd ever seen. Jessie guided me to our final destination—a long brownstone, three-story building that stretched for a block. It looked just what it was—a useless, abandoned 1900 federal building, now full of rats and other vermin, the only inhabitants of such a place. The smell was foul, too. It reminded me of rotten fish, only worse. I stopped outside what once must have been the main entrance, now barely closed with a couple of wooden bars, a lame replacement for the door that someone had stolen for better use.

"What is this?" I asked.

Jessie was one fast gal, I must give that to her. I was panting a little from the effort of keeping up with her, but tried to keep it from showing.

"This is Police Headquarters South," she said.

True, a faint sign above the door read *"lice th ...cinct,"* which might have meant that the building was a precinct house once upon a time, but I would have never guessed it. I had to remind myself that living persons and ghosts have different time perspectives. What to you appears to be a ruin of something is still fresh in the ghost's mind as it was when he lived, so we see things very differently. My ability to see dead people does not extend to viewing objects as they remember them, and that's always where my interaction with the deadies gets complex and prone to misunderstandings.

"All right. So how do we find this inspector of yours?"

"His office is on the second floor. Let's go up to see him."

Pulling away one of the bars that blocked the entrance was the work of a minute and we walked into the building, me treading gingerly for fear of falling through some hidden hole in the floor. The stairs were cast in concrete, so getting to the second floor wasn't hazardous and the corridor that opened before us got some daylight from broken windows in open offices—enough to be able to walk with some assurance. Around the middle of the corridor, Jessie stopped at a door and turned to me.

"Here it is," she announced.

The door still had a sign reading "Inspector T. R. Pratchet" on it and I went for the handle, but Jessie stopped me.

"Hey!" she yelled. "You need to knock."

I felt stupid, but I knocked on the door and was startled to hear a voice calling "Come in!"

I turned the handle and walked in. The room was in complete disarray, with paper spread all over the floor. Behind a dusty desk positioned in the darkest corner of the room sat a figure that I assumed was the ghost of Inspector Pratchet. He wore a jacket and a tie and, weirdest of all, a Homburg hat.

"Yes?" he said, looking annoyed.

"Good afternoon, Inspector," I said, using my best and most obsequious tone. "I wonder if we could have a moment of your time."

"I'm busy, here. Very busy," he said, barely lifting his gaze from some papers spread on the desk. "It has to be really important ... and urgent. Urgent and important, or come back some other day."

"It is, it is. You see, my friend Jessie here, said that you can help us."

"Oh, now I recognize you," he said, giving Jessie a dirty look. "Don't come pestering me again with that old shooting. I have nothing new for you. When I have any news you'll hear from me. Go now. Go! I'm busy," he said, and turned his attention again to the papers on his desk.

I stood there, considering which approach to take. Ghosts can be stubborn and we had started on the wrong foot. After a minute of silence he raised his head and gazed at me.

"You still here?" he complained.

"Yes, you see," I hastened to say while I had his attention, "this is not about the shooting. It's about a kidnapping."

"Kidnapping? Who's the victim? A child?"

I had got his attention and he got up from behind the desk.

"No, actually, it's an accountant. You see," I started to say but he checked me with a raised palm.

"You need to file a complaint. Let me find a form for that," he said, and started to search his desk. After a while he gave up the search. "I've run out of kidnapping forms. Go down to the sergeant on duty and get one, then after you fill-it in come back to me."

"Yes, but you see ..." I tried to argue, but I should've known better.

"Didn't you hear me?"

"Okay, thank you," I said, resigned.

"It's all right, come," Jessie whispered to me, and we left.

I closed the door behind us. I was exasperated and wanted to take it out on Jessie.

"A fat lot of good it was, meeting your inspector. You only wasted my time," I complained.

"Not at all. While you were talking to him I took a good look around, and what did I see?"

"What did you see?"

"Aha, you would like to know that, wouldn't you?"

"Of course I would like to know. Stop playing games with me, damn you!"

"No need to soil your mouth, you know. Let me tell you what I saw, okay?"

"Yes, do that," I said, raising my eyes to the ceiling.

"I saw a photograph of Inspector Pratchet shaking hands with another police officer. The legend of the photograph said, 'My friend and partner,' and the name of his partner was Ernest Malone. And do you know who Ernest Malone was?"

"Bugsy Malone's great-grandfather!" I exclaimed. "I take it all back. You're good. So now we know that Inspector Pratchet is connected with Bugsy Malone. That's a start, but it doesn't get us any closer to finding Randy, the accountant. And we have no idea of what they are up to."

"But it tells us that we should search this place. If they are in it together he might be here."

"I'm not sure that I am getting a clear idea. First, explain to me how you knew that we had to come here. I need some more information before I go ahead."

"That's very simple. My so-called friend, Lynn, the one who eloped with Randy, the accountant, she was always cooing to Inspector Pratchet. They got intimate after he arrested her one time for solicitation, and I suspected that she was giving him free services—that was before, you know ..."

I knew, dead people don't like to speak about the moment of their death.

"I see. So you put two and two together. But what now?"

"Now we go down and start looking around. We should search the ground floor and the basement. We might get lucky."

"Yeah, good idea. You're starting to make yourself useful."

Good idea? Lousy idea. I should have learned by now that going into the basements of unfamiliar buildings isn't the brightest move for me.

CHAPTER 7

The old police building had no electricity, of course, but I found an oil lamp behind the reception desk that still had some oil in it and I managed to light it.

"Come on," I said, "let's see if this place has anything useful for us."

I walked slowly down the stairs, putting the oil lamp forward as far as I could, to illuminate the steps with the little light it cast. At the bottom of the stairs a narrow corridor was in complete darkness, and the air was stale and oppressive. I stood in complete silence and listened.

"Do you hear it?" Jessie whispered.

"What is it?" I asked. It sounded like a low howl, like that of a dying dog.

"I don't know. Let me go ahead and see," she answered, and without waiting for my response she disappeared into the corridor. A minute later she was back. "There is someone lying on the floor in a cell at the end of the corridor. I couldn't see who it is."

"Let's go and find out," I said. I walked decidedly forward before my courage left me. I'm not a coward by any measure, but walking along dark corridors toward unidentified wailing individuals is no pleasure. Still, I had gone that far and I had to get to the bottom of it. Jessie, on her part, had no comments to offer. Ghosts always seem to be pretty unfazed by the possibility that a living person may be about to meet his doom, and Jessie was no exception.

Advancing along the corridor I saw a few cells with open barred doors, which had obviously been used in the past to keep felons, drunk and disorderly, before they were brought before a judge. The last cell was the one I was looking for. A figure was lying on the floor in a fetal position, his face hidden between his arms. A low lament was coming from it. The barred door of the cell was ajar and I opened it and stood at the entrance.

"Who is here? What's the matter with you?" I asked, speaking softly.

No answer came and the lament continued, so I took a step toward it and then I heard the clang of a door closing behind me. I turned quickly and saw that the door was locked and I realized that I was trapped inside. I turned again toward the man on the floor and the figure raised its head, revealing a face I had never seen before. Then, with a loud laugh, the apparition trembled and dissolved into thin air, leaving me all alone, locked in that cell.

"That was stupid of you, walking in here like that," came a reproachful comment from Jessie, who had showed up beside me. "Now you're a prisoner."

"Do you think I don't know that?" I answered angrily. "Why didn't you warn me?"

"When did you tell me to tell you what to do? I thought you knew what you were doing."

"So what now?" I asked. I don't mind admitting that right then I wasn't able to think straight.

"You tell me," she said, shrugging.

I slid against the wall and sat on the floor. I wasn't feeling particularly bright.

"Look here," I said, "You need to get me help. This oil lamp won't last for more than three–four hours and I can't stay in this cell in the dark; I'll go nuts."

"But who can I go to? Regular people don't see me outside the whorehouse. That's the only place where living people can see me. Except for you, of course."

"Go and get Jake," I said. "He will know what to do. He can manifest himself to living people. Go tell him the fix I'm in and he'll help me out."

"And what if I don't feel like it?" she said with a smug smile.

"What!" I cried. If she abandoned me that was the end.

"You haven't been kind to poor little Jessie," she said, getting closer and sitting on my lap. "Perhaps if you were to be nicer to me, I'd be happier about helping you," she added.

"Listen, Jessie," I said, in my best conciliatory tone, without succeeding in keeping the anguish out of my voce, "you know I appreciate you and I kept my word and got you out of the building, but if you abandon me now, I'm done for."

She got up quickly and smiled at me.

"Boy, you can't take a joke! Of course I'll get you out of this dump. Wait for me," she concluded, and then she disappeared, leaving me all alone to contemplate the result of my stupidity.

CHAPTER 8

This is how Jake told it to me, but knowing him I'm sure he embellished the story a lot. Anyway, here it is for what it's worth.

Jessie found Jake busy with one of the girls in an upper room.

"Hey, did you come to join us?" he asked.

"No. Stop that."

"Stop what?"

"Stop doing what you're doing and listen to me. Dave is in trouble."

Upon hearing that, Jake immediately became attentive and ignored the other girl's complaints, at which she upped and went off in a huff. (Later Jessie would say that it took her a long time and much nagging to make him pay attention at all, which sounds a lot more like my friend Jake.)

"What kind of trouble? Define trouble."

"He's locked in a basement cell with no light, food, or water and probably about to be killed or left to die there. I call that 'trouble.' He said that I should tell you and you'll be able to help him."

"He must've gone soft in the head. He should know that I can't leave this building because I'm sitting in for you—"

"I'll stay and let you go," Jessie said, cutting him short.

"But even if you do that, I can't go anywhere on my own. I need to be attached to somebody and I have nobody to be attached to."

"But if I release you from this building, don't you have to go back to your original one, the one you can't stay more than a hundred feet away from?"

"Hmm, you have a point. I'll tell you what we'll do. I'll wait for someone to pass by in the street and when he is close enough you'll release me and I'll get attached to him. Then I'll find a way to make him go where I need to be."

"All right, but tell Dave that he must come back and get me out again. He owes it to me, okay? That's why I don't want him to die in that basement," Jessie said, pointedly.

"Don't play the hard woman, baby. You can't fool Uncle Jake. You could have let Dave rot in that basement and me stuck in this brothel—which, incidentally, I don't know that I would have objected to—instead of going to all the trouble of trying to save him. That tells me that you have a soft spot for Dave."

"Don't be ridiculous ... well, maybe a little. Enough chat now, let's get moving! Memorize the address where Dave is being held," she added, and gave it to him.

Jake and Jessie stood by the window and waited for a suitable passerby. The first one was an old woman and they agreed that using her would be too dangerous. She might freak out or have a fit or something. Luckily, the second one was a young man with long hair and a long stride. As soon as he passed below the window Jessie said "Now," and Jake found himself on the pavement, facing the young man.

"Pardon me, sir," he said, addressing him.

"Where did you come from? A moment ago you weren't there. And why are you wearing strange clothes? I only sniffed a little, but you must be a hallucination. They surely sold me bad stuff. Am I going to die?" he asked in sudden anguish.

"No, Mate, don't worry. You're okay. Forget my clothes for now. I need your help getting somewhere," said Jake, trying to sound soothing.

"I'm not going anywhere with you. Figure that! You *are* a hallucination. Nobody speaks like you. Go away."

The young man closed his eyes and started walking again. After a minute or so, and after walking into a lamppost, he opened his eyes again and found himself face-to-face with Jake, who decided to take a different approach.

"Listen to me, Mate. I am Captain Nemesis and I'm here to take you to hell. If you don't help me you will end up in the eternal flames. Now get moving."

Unfortunately, Jake's approach obtained the opposite of what he had hoped. The young man remained seated on the ground, where he had fallen after colliding with the lamppost, took his face in his hands and started to shake. Right then, a yellow cab stopped at the curb.

"Do you folks need to go anywhere?" asked the driver.

Brilliant, Jake thought. *Why didn't I think of a cab to begin with?*

"Yes, Mate. Forget him, he isn't going anywhere, but I need you to take me to the docks. Can you open the door for me, please? I have a hand condition."

When Jake told me about it, I felt pride that I had managed to teach him not to spook people by walking through doors as he used to do when I first started to go out with him. The taxi driver obliged him and Jake attached himself to him, leaving the young man to sob on the ground. When they reached the pub, however, he forgot how to behave and, in haste, jumped out of the cab. To the astounded driver he said, "Wait for the barman, he'll pay you," and once again walked through the entrance door to the pub.

Inside, the bartender barely raised an eyebrow. Jake approached him and shouted, "Dave's in danger, get moving!"

That statement put things in motion in the federal building. The taxi driver was paid and a SWAT team, always ready for action, was called upon to rescue their landlord.

Meanwhile, not knowing that things were in motion, I sat, thoroughly miserable, watching my oil lamp flicker in the otherwise complete darkness and blaming myself for my stupidity. The sound of boots and the light coming from the corridor brought the rose back to my cheeks. At that moment, Jake's voice was the most beautiful sound I had ever heard.

"Got yourself into trouble, Mate, haven't you?" he said, showing up beside me as I jumped to my feet.

"Go to the end of the cell, Mr. Callaghan, while we blast this lock away," said a Fed I had seen before. A low boom ensued and then the door swung open.

We all got to the ground floor and I thanked the team leader for rescuing me, requested that we postpone the paperwork to justify the activity to a later time, and asked him if they had found anybody else in the building.

"We combed it from top to bottom and there is nobody else here. You were the only one in the building," he said.

"Let's go home, Jake," I said. "I need a shower and then we must think what to do next."

At the door, I turned one last time to look at the building. Inspector Pratchet was at the top of the stairs, a grin on his face. My list of ghosts to get even with was growing longer.

CHAPTER 9

A hot shower usually cleans my head and helps me put the pieces of the puzzle I'm currently working on in order, but this time I came out of the shower as confused as I had gone in. None of the pieces seemed to fit the others, and I hadn't even started to see something resembling a whole picture. Dressed only in my trunks, I grabbed a beer from the fridge and went to sit in my usual armchair. Jake, who was gazing out the window, turned to me and lifted a disapproving eyebrow.

"Mate, you got yourself into a big mess, this time," he said.

"Yes, thanks for pointing that out to me. I don't know how I would have figured that out without you," I said.

"No need to be sarcastic, you know? It's not my fault."

"No, it isn't, but you are not being helpful."

"I got you out of that basement, didn't I? Doesn't that count as being helpful?"

Jake had a point. I was sore at myself and I had no business taking it out on him.

"I'm sorry," I said, "you did save my ass."

"Again, I should point out."

"Yeah, I haven't forgotten the first time we met. But what good is it, being out of that basement if I don't know what to do next?"

"Man, aren't you gloomy! Perhaps you should loosen up a bit and spend some time with that Jessie gal. She has the hots for you."

"Don't be ridiculous. Ghosts don't get the hots for living people."

"No? So am I not a ghost? Haven't you been listening to me for the past two years, or do you think I'm faking it?"

"You're special," I said.

"Not in that sense. Believe me, you mean something to her."

"Forget it for now. Did you learn anything of interest in that whorehouse, besides having fun with the ladies?"

"Not really. I tried to talk to that madam, but she kept her distance. The way they keep that place is a disgrace. Her pimp must've been lazy. Anyway, she wouldn't even speak to me and, except for once, I never saw her around."

I sat up and almost dropped the bottle of beer on my lap.

"You're a genius, Jake!" I yelled.

"Am I? Of course I know I am, but why are you telling me this now?"

"You'll see. I'll get dressed and then I have things to do. Get ready," I added, forgetting that ghosts have no corporeal needs and are always ready.

First of all I had to consult the Feds' database. Jake bitched a bit, I guess because he thought that I might leave him at the station, but after I swore on my girlfriend that I would take him with me, he agreed to keep quiet while I drove to the pub. Inside, I went down the stairs to the computer room that my tenants had graciously agreed to let me use from time to time. I keyed in "Inspector T. R. Pratchet" and a short paragraph came up on the screen. It said "T. R. Pratchet: Under federal investigation for trafficking and colluding with nationwide criminal organizations. Allegedly participated in attacks meant to maintain his partners' control of the prostitution scene. Accused of murder by anonymous information—never tried. Deceased: Shot by relative of alleged victim."

So this Pratchet was one of the bad guys, a rotten apple. That meant that he almost certainly had a hand in my unpleasant stay in the cellar. But if Jesse knew it—and she had to know it—why did she take me to him? He was clearly not going to help us. Jessie obviously wasn't trying to harm me, but sometimes the thought processes of ghosts are tortuous; there had to be a reason for her bringing me to see Pratchet, and I'd better find out what it was.

My next stop was one I wasn't looking forward to. Eberhard Ussberg, nicknamed "Eber Ass," hated my guts. We had met for the first time at a summer camp when we were fifteen years old, and he has accused me ever since of being the one who pinned him down to his bed while others pushed his hands into ice water and made him piss in his pants. If you ask me about it, I'll take the fifth, but I can tell you that he had it coming to him. We discovered that he had a bag packed with M&M's and that he was chewing them silently at night under his blanket, to avoid sharing. He was a fat, ugly boy then, and was still fat and ugly now as a grown-up, but he also had made chief of police. He was constantly looking for ways to take my license away and had almost succeeded on one occasion.

I waited for Eber Ass's secretary to be busy at the phone and then I pushed in unannounced. I found him sitting at his desk, munching on a candy bar.

"What the hell! Who let you in?" he yelled as soon as he managed to swallow the last bite.

"Good day to you too, Chief," I said, with my best smile. "I bring you fame and happiness," I added.

I turned around to see what Jake was up to, and I saw that he hadn't come into the room with me. Better that way for the time being.

"How do you dare barge in like that? We'll hang you for this," he said.

"Oh, cool down. They don't hang you for visiting an old friend."

"Old friend my foot! What do you want?"

"I have a proposition for you," I said, and I seated myself in one of the comfortable leather chairs that my taxes had paid for. "This is election year and you know as well as I do that, so far, your performance has been rather poor. You could do with a big bust with lots of good publicity. I bring you that big bust."

His eyes narrowed to slits and he eyed me in silence. I could almost read what was going on in that thing between his ears that passes for a brain—he was weighing his loathing for me against the mirage of a big case with good press, of which he hadn't seen much until then.

"Tell me more," he said at last.

"I can't give you the details yet. First we need to talk to the mayor and get his cooperation. Then I'll fill you in on all the details."

"I can't go to the mayor and talk to him about something I have no clue about," he complained. His demeanor made it clear that he was on board already, and damn the details.

"No mayor, no dice. You don't need to take the blame for it. I'll do the talking."

"Let me make a phone call and see if the mayor can see us."

"All right. While you do that, I need to see what happened to a friend of mine who is coming along."

I found Jake sitting on the secretary's desk. She was slumped in her chair and breathed heavily.

"I didn't do anything, I swear," he said as I approached. "I just asked her to open her blouse a little and she fainted."

"You underestimate your powers, Jake," I said patiently. He tends to forget that he is translucent and that sensitive people may take that badly. "Now go to the other end of the room and wait for me, okay?"

Jake obliged and parked himself out of sight of the secretary's desk. I went back inside.

"The mayor will see us now," said Eber Ass. He got up and I followed. Passing by his secretary's desk, he threw a half-hearted "Sleeping on the job" stink. He was famous for being mean to his staff, but clearly right then his heart wasn't in it.

I had never been in the mayor's office before and expected something more stylish. It was roomy and full of plaques and trophies, but it was not impressive. The mayor himself was not impressive. A little squirt with short hair and graying temples in a gray suit added up to a gray mayor. Still, I only needed him to do a few staple acts that even the grayest of mayors could do.

"Yes, Chief. You said that this is urgent enough to disrupt my busy schedule today, so let's have it."

As if we didn't know that his busy schedule amounted to a couple of phone calls and a round of golf. Politicians are so pathetic that you don't know whether to despise or to pity them. Eber Ass squirmed uncomfortably in his chair and decided to pass the bucket to me, which was fine since he couldn't have done anything right.

"Sir, I'll let Mister Callaghan explain it to you. He has all the details and has been cooperating with our department on this delicate matter."

That was a good one, "cooperating." *Perhaps this is the beginning of a beautiful friendship*, I thought, laughing to myself at the notion.

"Sir, we have identified a broad criminal operation headed by one Bugsy Malone," I said, using my most obsequious tone of voice.

"This Malone individual is a well-known racketeer that our department has been trying to stop for years," Eber Ass added helpfully. He knew how to spot a cue, I had to give him that.

"What kind of criminal operation would that be?" asked the mayor. I'd been expecting that question.

"A large one. Very large. It has to do with prostitution and other major crimes," I said. "When, with your help, we stop him, it will have broad repercussions on the crime scene of our city. Very broad. They will be talking about it for months."

"What can I help you with?"

"It's very simple. To uncover central parts of this operation, we will need two demolition orders, which are entirely in your power. One for an old, empty government building, to be executed immediately since timing is of the essence, and the other for a building on Marlborough Road, to be executed only if and after I personally authorize it. That's all."

"And you will mention my role, when reporting to the public on this operation ... ?"

"Of course, sir. Without your help we could never win the war on crime, isn't that so, Chief?" I added, pushing my elbow into Eber Ass's side.

"True, true. We must make sure to give the mayor his rightful credit. We are a team, all of us," Eber Ass said dutifully.

"Give me the details," said the mayor. "You will have the orders within the hour."

We waited for the papers in a small waiting room beside the mayor's office. Jake, who had waited outside unobtrusively while we spoke with the mayor, had now joined and was sitting moodily at one end of the oval table.

"This isn't fun," he complained.

I knew what his beef was. I had forbidden him to talk to the mayor's secretary, a quite presentable, scantily dressed wench, and he was lamenting an opportunity lost. He understood that it wasn't a good time to explain him away to every secretary he gave fits to, but wasn't liking it all the same. I'd already had a hard time explaining him to Eber Ass, who wasn't entirely convinced that I wasn't pulling his leg, and I didn't need any more trouble. After a brief argument, however, he had decided to let it go and to ignore Jake altogether, which suited me fine.

A knock on the door announced the arrival of our papers. I took them from the secretary's hand before she managed to get a view of the room, thanked her and as soon as she left we sneaked out.

CHAPTER 10

Now that the time for action had come, I could only hope that I was right. If I wasn't, it would all blow up in my face, and I didn't want to think of the consequences. Eber Ass and a SWAT team waited a block await for me to whistle them in. I had to convince him to wait with them instead of coming with me as he had hoped to do. I guess that he wanted to protect his investment and to make sure that I wasn't pulling a fast one on him, but seeing me talking to the deadies, whom he wouldn't see, wasn't doable. He would immediately conclude that I was off my rocker.

I pushed the door open and there was the madam, with an unwelcoming twist on her face.

"We only entertain paying guests," she said. "Please leave now."

"You know what this is?" I asked, pulling out the mayor's order. "It is a demolition order for this building. One more peep out of you and down goes this joint."

"He will do it too, believe him," Jake added. "He's as mean as they come."

Jake's intervention made me smile, but I kept the smile to myself. I don't think that ghosts can pale, but she did the next thing to it, or so it seemed to me. She gave me a poisonous look and moved aside.

"Stay here and don't get in the way," I ordered, and walked in.

In the sitting room, the same girls waited in exactly the same position as I had seen them the first time. Jessie gave me a startled look but said nothing. The two girls who had ignored me the first time still ignored me and continued to whisper to one another and giggle, but this time I wasn't fooled. I walked up to them and stood before them.

"Which one of you is Lynn?" I asked.

They gazed at me in silence and said nothing.

"I know that one of you is she, so you may as well tell me."

Until that very moment I had been afraid that I had made a blunder, but then the one on the right raised her gaze, looked straight at me and said, "I'm Lynn." A weight fell off my shoulders.

"Hello, Lynn," I said. Before getting down to business I needed to create a rapport with her. I never forget that when meeting a ghost for the first time. The one time that I forgot it, the ghost clammed up and I never got anything from it.

"Hello," she answered demurely.

"I need your help. Will you help me?"

"What do you want?"

"I need to know where Randy is. Randolph. Can you tell me that?"

Her gaze left my face and she looked around the room, as if to find there an answer to my question. Then, she turned back to me and murmured, "Downstairs."

"How do I go downstairs?" I asked. When you are dealing with a shy ghost, you need to be patient and take small steps.

"Under the stairway. There is a little door."

"Thank you, Lynn," I said gently, and turned to leave.

I almost got to the door when Jessie showed up in my way. "Dave ..." she started to say, but I cut her short.

"Later, Jessie. No time now," I said.

I ran to the door and as soon as I got outside I waved my hands. A bunch of blue-uniformed men appeared as if out of nowhere, with Eber Ass at their head. He reached me and asked, panting heavily, "What now?"

"We need to go downstairs. The entrance is concealed under the stairway. Be careful because we don't know what to expect."

Eber nodded in assent and signaled his men to follow him. There were more than a dozen clad in protective armor, and that should have sufficed. As soon as the last police officer got inside I followed them and waited by the door until someone called the "all clear," and then I ducked under the stairs and through the small door that was now open and down to a smelly basement.

The scene that revealed itself to me was more than expected. Bugsy Malone was on the floor, handcuffed, as was our friend Randolph. The room was filled with printing machines and with forged dollars. A ghost I had seen before—he was the one that had tricked me into the cell in the police station basement—stood in one corner and inspected the scene. Of course I was the only one to see him and I walked up to him.

"You're the pimp, right?" I asked point blank. I needed no cooperation from this one so no need to be polite. It was just curiosity.

"I'm Susan's husband," he said.

"Just out of curiosity, why were you helping these guys invade your home?"

"The boss, Bugsy, he threatened to demolish the place if we didn't help him, so we did."

"Were you the one that popped up in my shower pretending to be Randy?"

"How did you know?" Ghosts usually don't show surprise, but this one did.

"I'm a detective. I detect. Why did you do it?"

"Bugsy wanted you to think that Ralph had been kidnapped, to confuse you."

"Okay, that makes sense," I said, and walked to where Randolph was lying cuffed, his face to the floor.

"Who were you talking to?" asked Eber.

"Nobody. Just talking to myself. What have you got here?"

"Talking to yourself ... I always thought that you were crazy. But this time you were right. These gentlemen here," he added, kicking first Randolph and then Bugsy, "were printing fake money and then laundering it through Randolph's boss's bank accounts that our friend Randolph here managed."

I had one point on which I wasn't clear and to which I needed an answer. I knelt beside Randolph and pulled him by the hair to make him pay attention.

"Why did you make that phone call from this place, I'm curious to know? That's what got you into trouble."

"I needed to disappear. I needed everybody to think that I had been kidnapped. How could I know that you would trace the call to this place? I used the phone that Malone had installed in the cellar and it was supposed to be unlisted."

"This is a good catch, Callaghan," Eber Ass said, kicking the pair once again. "I may even forgive you for that thing at the camp on account of that. Take them out of here!" he yelled to his men. "This place stinks. I'm going out and back to the office. Later there will be a press conference. Are you coming?"

"In a while. I've got some other things to do first," I said. I hate leaving loose ends, and I had a bunch of them to take care of.

Upstairs, Jake was chatting with the girls in the kitchen. I had told them to stay out of the way, because I didn't need some police officer to see them and freak out. They were visible to living people only when they were in the display room or upstairs, so the kitchen wasn't a danger zone. They did not appear at all concerned with all the commotion that went on down below, with the exception of Jessie. She was seated at the far end of the sofa, looking pensive and, upon seeing me coming in, she got up and waited.

"So," I said and waited, but she didn't respond. "You were playing games with me, after all."

"I was looking out for the girls," she said, without looking straight at me. "But at the same time I was looking out for you."

"How come?"

"Susan had promised that she would let me and the other girls go, if they wanted to, if I helped her to keep you away from Randy. That's why I took you to the old police station. I thought that you would see that there was nothing to be found and would give up. That's all there was to it."

"You could have left me in that cell and your job would have been done," I pointed out.

"I didn't know that Bugsy Malone would be there at the same time, nor that he planned to imprison you. And I didn't want you to get hurt," she said, looking quickly away.

"Look at me," I ordered, and she returned her gaze to my face. "I know that you are telling the truth. Thank you."

She smiled and nodded.

"I'm sorry I misled you, but I'm happy that you're okay."

"All right. Now let's go and talk to Susan," I said, and went to the foyer, which was now quiet after the last police officer had left. Susan was standing at the door, as usual, and I walked up to her, followed by Jessie.

"Susan," I said, "I demand that you release Jessie and the other girls of their contract. They must be free to go if they want to."

"I don't think so. How am I to run this establishment if I lose my best girls?"

"I've spoken with the girls," Jessie intervened. "Most of them will stay on, by choice, not by force."

I had no patience for Susan and wasn't going to sweet talk her into releasing the girls.

"Demolition, remember?" I said, waving the order before her again. "Unless you release them immediately, down goes this building and everybody will be released. Do you prefer it that way?"

Susan looked at me with open loathing, but knew that she was licked.

"Go!" she said, gazing at the floor.

"I don't think we got it. Say it clearly," I demanded. "And play no games with us. I'm keeping this demolition order and I can use it any time."

Susan once again eyed me with hatred, but I know that hatred can't kill me.

"You are free to go, Jessie. I release you of your contract. I release everybody. All the girls are released and if they want to, they may go. You may go. Go!"

Jessie smiled a bright smile. She suddenly looked brighter and stronger.

"Thank you, Dave. Thank you so much!"

"You're welcome. I promised it to you. So now you'll be gone, I guess."

"Yes, in a little while."

"If you can make the time, I'd like you to come with me to see something. A quick thing."

"I'll come wherever you want me to," she said.

"Jake!" I cried. "We need to go."

Jake's head popped out of the wall next to us. He likes to do theatrical things; it's part of his charm.

"Hmm, Mate. I'm kind of in a middle of something. Could you come back for me later?"

"As long as you're not in a hurry," I said, knowing well he wasn't. "I'll pick you up when I'm free."

"No hurry whatever, Mate. Take your time," he said, and his

head disappeared through the wall.

CHAPTER 11

The mayor had kept his promise. Where the old brownstone building of the defunct police precinct had once stood, now there was only rubble. I approached it slowly with Jessie floating alongside me.

"How did this happen?" she asked. She sounded amazed and smiled broadly.

"I made it happen," I said. "I thought it best to clean up after myself."

"Look!" she said.

I gazed up at the top of the rubble and there was Inspector Pratchet, standing alone in his stupid Homburg hat. He shook his fist at me a couple of times and then puff, he went, hopefully for good. Jessie smiled again and giggled—a funny thing for a ghost to do.

"I thought you would be pleased," I said. "I knew you would want to see this before you go."

"Why did you think that?"

"He was one of the killers, wasn't he?"

Jessie turned around for a moment and waited before responding. I knew that I had made her go back to the moment of her death and that was hard on her. After a few seconds she turned back and gazed straight at me.

"He wasn't one of the shooters, but he was there. He watched them do it, laughing. So yes, thank you for letting me see that."

"I guessed that he was involved, but I didn't know exactly how. Thanks for sharing."

"You are very good at guessing! I don't understand how you concluded that Lynn was one of the girls at the house. How could you know?"

"Actually, I didn't really know. It was something that Jake said to me that made me remember that I had read that the shooting at the house had left eight dead. I had counted six girls plus Susan and, at first, I bought into the story that the missing one was Lynn. But then I realized that someone else had to be involved, a man. Someone had to run the place, to look after it and to give you girls protection—not very efficiently, as we have seen. So, if there was a man among the dead, all the girls were accounted for and Lynn had to be one of them. Simple."

"You are very intelligent, Dave Callaghan," she said, "and kind."

She raised a hand and caressed my cheek, and this time I didn't shy away from her touch. It felt weird but real and it had a meaning. She took a step back and gazed into my eyes. She had started to flicker and I knew what was coming.

"I'll miss you, Dave. I hope you'll miss me too, at least a little."

"I will," I managed to say before she disappeared without a sound.

I didn't feel like going to see Eber Ass. I'd had enough of him and, as it always happens when a case is resolved, I felt pretty much emptied of strength. A good drink in the company of friends was what I really needed. I went back to the whorehouse and, making my way through the yellow police tape, I reached the entrance and yelled for Jake. I hoped that he would keep me company while I drank myself to sleep. As if I didn't know him ...

"Mate, I'm still in the middle of the same something. Can't you come back tomorrow?"

"I'll come back when I do," I sighed. "Have fun."

So it was Eber Ass or going home alone. Pathetic. But then I remembered Dolly. How could I have forgotten her? She was the answer. I found a nearby phone and called her.

"Hi," her deep, sensual voice greeted me. "Where have you been?"

"It's a long story. You'll read about it in the news. I'm coming to see you, okay?"

"Sure," she said, and hung up.

I hailed a cab and went straight to her apartment. She opened the door and gave me a welcome kiss, which I really needed. I looked at her. She was stunning in a flaming evening dress.

"Wow!" I said. "You're all dressed up. For me?"

"Yes," she said. "It's lucky that you called on time, otherwise we would have missed the opening."

"Opening? What are you talking about?"

"You forgot," she said. She shook her head in disapproval. "It doesn't matter, really. The important thing is that you got here in time. I told you I have tickets for *La Traviata*. If we leave now we'll get to the opera house before they close the doors."

I told you. I'm straight up cursed.

Meet the Author

Kfir Luzzatto is the author of twelve novels, several short stories, and seven non-fiction books. Kfir was born and raised in Italy and moved to Israel as a teenager. He acquired the love for the English language from his father, a former U.S. soldier, a voracious reader, and a prolific writer. Kfir has a Ph.D. in chemical engineering and works as a patent attorney. He lives in Omer, Israel, with his full-time partner, Esther, and their four children, Michal, Lilach, Tamar, and Yonatan.

In pursuit of his interest in the mind-body connection, Kfir was certified as a Clinical Hypnotherapist by the Anglo European College of Therapeutic Hypnosis.

Kfir has published extensively in the professional and general press over the years. For almost four years, he wrote a weekly "Patents" column in Globes (Israel's financial newspaper). His popular guide, *FUN WITH PATENTS—The Irreverent Guide for the Investor, the Entrepreneur, and the Inventor*, was published in 2016. He is an HWA (Horror Writers Association) and ITW (International Thriller Writers) member.

You can visit Kfir's website and read his blog at www.kfirluzzatto.com. Follow him on Twitter (@KfirLuzzatto) and friend him on Facebook (https://www.facebook.com/ KfirLuzzattoAuthor/).